The Sign
of the Falcon

Nancy and her friends emerged from the tunnel in Central Park and continued down the path. After a few minutes they came to a large lawn full of sunbathers and picnickers.

Nancy stopped and looked around. "Do you guys see that gray-haired guy?"

"In this crowd? No way." George sighed. "He might not even have stayed on this path. He could have taken a detour."

"I think we've lost him for good," Nancy murmured in frustration. "I guess we'd better give up and head back over to the Imperial Hotel." She shook her head. "I still don't get it, though. If the gray-haired man is one of Dad's kidnappers, why is he following *us*? It doesn't make sense."

Bess frowned. "I just had an awful idea, Nan. What if he wants to kidnap you, too?"

Nancy Drew
Mystery Stories

Available from MINSTREL Books

NANCY DREW ®

130

THE SIGN
OF THE FALCON

CAROLYN KEENE

A
MINSTREL®
BOOK

Published by POCKET BOOKS
New York   London   Toronto   Sydney   Tokyo   Singapore

A MINSTREL PAPERBACK *Original*

A Minstrel Book published by
POCKET BOOKS, a division of Simon & Schuster Inc.
1230 Avenue of the Americas, New York, NY 10020

Copyright © 1996 by Simon & Schuster Inc.
Produced by Mega-Books, Inc.

ISBN: 0-671-50508-4

First Minstrel Books printing February 1996

10 9 8 7 6 5 4 3 2 1

Cover art by Craig Nelson

Printed in the U.S.A.

Contents

THE SIGN
OF THE FALCON

1

Dad's Missing!

"It's so great to be back in New York," Bess Marvin remarked, staring out the cab window at the majestic Manhattan skyline. Then she glanced at her friend Nancy Drew, who was sitting next to her. "I wish it didn't have to be under these circumstances, though," she added softly.

Eighteen-year-old Nancy nodded, her blue eyes troubled. Usually, the ride from LaGuardia Airport into Manhattan filled her with excitement and anticipation, but not today. "Me, too," she said. "I mean, we've been here on cases before, but not one involving my own father."

On Nancy's other side, George Fayne, Bess's dark-haired cousin, put on a cheerful smile. "I bet we'll find your dad right away," she said brightly.

"It's probably just a mix-up," Bess added. "You

1

know, like he left town for a few days for some R and R and forgot to tell anyone."

"I hope so," Nancy murmured. Inside, however, she knew something was terribly wrong.

Carson Drew had come to New York four days ago on a business trip—and vanished into thin air. The first alarm had come the night before—Wednesday night—from his sister, Eloise Drew. Eloise, who lived in Greenwich Village, was supposed to meet Nancy's dad for dinner at seven. When he didn't show up at the restaurant, she called his hotel, the Imperial. The manager informed her that he wasn't in his room and hadn't been there for a while. Worried, Eloise then called Nancy.

Nancy had contacted the Imperial Hotel herself and pressed the manager, Mr. Lambert, for details of her father's comings and goings. Mr. Lambert explained that Mr. Drew had checked into the hotel on Sunday, the day he arrived in New York. But while Mr. Drew had slept in his room on Sunday and Monday nights, he definitely hadn't slept there on Tuesday; the bed hadn't been touched. Furthermore, he hadn't picked up the messages and faxes that had been piling up for him since Tuesday morning.

Nancy's next call had been to her father's secretary, Ms. Hanson.

"I haven't heard from your dad since Tuesday morning," Ms. Hanson had told Nancy. "I thought it was kind of strange—whenever he goes out of town, he usually checks in with me two or three times a day. Plus, I sent some important faxes to his hotel late Tuesday afternoon, and he never acknowledged them."

That was Wednesday night. It was now Thursday. First thing that morning Nancy had decided to come to New York, with her friends George and Bess in tow. An amateur detective, Nancy often used their help on cases. She was determined to use all of her detective skills to find her father. She'd lost her mother when she was just three, so he was the only parent she had ever really known. There was no way she was going to lose him, too.

"Nancy?" Bess's voice cut into her thoughts. "I just know we're going to find your dad right away. And as soon as we do, we can celebrate by having a real New York vacation. We can go clothes shopping—I got the names of a bunch of cool new stores from my favorite magazine, *Bellissima*. Oh, and I want to try that new restaurant where all the waiters and waitresses are on roller skates. Plus, we have to take in a Broadway show, maybe a musical . . ."

"Maybe we could catch a Mets game, too," George spoke up. "You like baseball, right, Nan? And there's a 10K race in Central Park on Sunday."

"You want to exercise while you're here?" Bess said, aghast. "Why?"

Despite her preoccupied mood, Nancy couldn't help but grin. She never stopped marveling at how different the two cousins were. Aside from their physical appearances—Bess was short, blond, and forever dieting, and George was tall, brunette, and athletic—their personalities were as different as night and day.

The cabdriver turned around. "So are you girls visiting someone in New York?"

"My father—" Nancy began, then her voice caught in her throat.

"We're visiting her father's sister," Bess said quickly. "That's where we're headed now."

Trying to keep her emotions at bay, Nancy opened the window a crack and took a deep breath. The balmy April breeze stirred her reddish blond hair. As the cab sped across the Queensboro Bridge, she stared at the steel blue waters of the East River and the cars jammed bumper to bumper on the FDR Drive just ahead.

Manhattan was an island of over a million people, she mused. Where among them was her father?

"Nancy!"

Standing in the doorway of her apartment, Eloise Drew wrapped Nancy in a tearful hug.

"Hi, Aunt Eloise." Pulling back, Nancy felt a pang in her heart as she studied her aunt's face, so like her father's. Today it was lined with worry.

Eloise hugged George and Bess, then picked up one of the girls' bags and waved everyone into the

4

living room. "Are you hungry?" she said. "I got some cookies and fruit from the deli around the corner. And excuse the mess—I haven't had a chance to pick up, with all of this happening."

Nancy glanced around. As always, her aunt's apartment looked inviting and homey. All around there were big, soft chairs and pillows, piles of interesting-looking magazines, and vases of colorful spring flowers: daffodils, hyacinths, and tulips.

Nancy smiled at her aunt. "Mess? What mess? The place looks wonderful."

Bess tossed her long blond hair over her shoulders. "Definitely. If you want to see a *real* mess, check out my room at home."

When they'd all sat down in the living room, Nancy turned to her aunt. "So, Aunt Eloise—did you get a chance to talk to the police about Dad?"

"I went down to the station and filed a missing-persons report this morning," Eloise replied, passing a plate of cookies and fruit around. "Officer Jordan—the man I talked to—said they'd get on the case as soon as they can." She frowned. "He warned me that their department is very overloaded right now. Of course, I gave him a piece of my mind, but who knows if that'll get results?"

George took a banana from the plate. "Did they have any idea what might have happened to Mr. Drew?" she asked Eloise.

Eloise shook her head. "Not without gathering more facts," she said. "Speaking of gathering

5

facts, I called all the hospitals to see if Carson or anyone fitting his description had checked in in the last forty-eight hours. I didn't have any luck."

"At least we can rule that out, anyway," Nancy said, relieved.

Bess bit into a peanut butter cookie. "So what's our plan for the rest of the afternoon, Nan?"

Nancy considered. "I think you and Aunt Eloise should stay here and make phone calls," she said. "For starters, call all the airlines and the train, bus, and car rental companies in town and see if Dad might have used them in the last few days."

"Sounds good," Eloise said. "I've got keys to my neighbor's apartment—I'm watering her plants while she's away on vacation. I'm sure she wouldn't mind if I used her phone. That way, Bess can use the one in here, and we'll go a lot faster."

"Great." Nancy pulled a piece of paper out of her jeans pocket. "In the meantime, George, you and I will hit the streets. Dad's secretary gave me the number of a lawyer named Miguel Lopez— Dad had lunch with him on Monday. Mr. Lopez might be able to tell us something about Dad's whereabouts. I also want to go by the Imperial Hotel to check out Dad's room."

Eloise grabbed Nancy's hand and squeezed it. "I'm so glad you girls are here. With all your experience as detectives, we should find Carson in no time."

Nancy squeezed back. She could tell that her

aunt was trying to sound brave and cheerful. "I'm sure we will," she said encouragingly.

"I met your father for lunch on Monday at one o'clock, at a restaurant around the corner," Miguel Lopez told Nancy. "We're working on opposite sides of a case, and we had some matters to go over."

Nancy and George were in Mr. Lopez's office, on the Upper West Side of Manhattan. The young, dark-haired lawyer was sitting behind a desk cluttered with files and old Styrofoam coffee cups.

Nancy leaned forward in her chair. "What kind of case?" she asked him curiously.

"A malpractice suit. I'm afraid I'm not at liberty to discuss the details." Mr. Lopez picked up a pencil and tapped it lightly against his desk calendar. "I've been trying to get in touch with your father for the last few days, Ms. Drew. He was supposed to send me some very important documents by Tuesday at five, and they never came. And here it is Thursday already."

"Did Mr. Drew happen to tell you what his plans were for the rest of the week?" George spoke up.

Mr. Lopez shook his head. "No. We talked about the case—that's all." He added, "Come to think of it, as he left, he asked me for directions to the City Hall area. Maybe he had some business down there?"

7

Nancy frowned. That was odd—Ms. Hanson hadn't said anything about her father having an appointment downtown near City Hall on Monday afternoon.

After asking the lawyer several more questions, Nancy and George thanked him and left. Outside, George turned to Nancy. "Tuesday seems to be a key day," she commented. "Ms. Hanson said that she hasn't heard from your dad since Tuesday morning. And the manager at his hotel said that he slept there Sunday and Monday, but not Tuesday."

Nancy nodded. "It seems as if Dad went somewhere that afternoon—but where?"

The girls took the subway down to the midtown area. It was nearly six o'clock when they emerged from the Rockefeller Center station. Aboveground, the Avenue of the Americas was lined with tall skyscrapers, and the sidewalks were jammed with people just getting off from work. The rush-hour traffic blared and rumbled, while neon signs and streetlights glittered against the dusky blue, twilit sky.

They soon reached the Imperial Hotel, an elegant ten-story building just off the avenue. At the front desk a young clerk smiled at the girls. "Can I help you ladies?"

"I'd like to see Mr. Lambert, if he's here," Nancy told him.

"Certainly." The clerk picked up the phone and spoke into it. Seconds later a portly, middle-aged man emerged from behind a closed door. He pushed his wire-rimmed glasses up his nose and studied Nancy and George. "Yes? What can I do for you?"

Nancy introduced herself. "We spoke on the phone last night about my father, Carson Drew. I was wondering if we could take a look at his room. It might help us figure out where he is."

"Of course," Mr. Lambert replied. "But first, I'll need to see some ID."

Nancy dug into her purse and produced her driver's license. Mr. Lambert glanced at it, handed it back to her, then reached for a key labeled Suite 312 on a hook. "Right this way," he said to the girls.

As they crossed the lobby and went into the elevator, Mr. Lambert said, "I don't know if I told you on the phone, but your father paid for his suite through Saturday."

"No, you didn't mention that," Nancy replied. "If we haven't . . ." Her voice wavered slightly. "If we haven't found him by then, I'll be sure to clear out his things."

George put a hand on Nancy's arm. "Think positive, Nan," she murmured.

The elevator reached the third floor, and the doors swooshed open. Nancy, George, and Mr. Lambert stepped out. A plush carpeted hall stretched ahead, with a dozen doors on either side. At the end was a door with a bright red Exit sign over it.

"Mr. Drew's suite is the last one on the right,"

Mr. Lambert said. "It's one of our deluxe . . ." He paused and frowned. "Wait a second—what's that woman doing there? That's Mr. Drew's suite!"

Nancy followed Mr. Lambert's glance. Outside the last door on the right stood a woman wearing a brown raincoat, a matching hat pulled low, gloves, and red cat's-eye-shaped sunglasses. Her hand clutched the doorknob.

Nancy gasped. "She's trying to break in!" she cried out.

2

A Mysterious List

Without wasting another second, Nancy started down the hall, followed by Mr. Lambert and George. Before they got very far, the woman turned and spotted them. She raised one gloved hand to her lips, then whirled around and took off in the other direction.

"Wait a second, miss! Excuse me!" Mr. Lambert called out. But the woman ignored him and charged through the door marked Exit. It slammed behind her with a loud bang.

Mr. Lambert stopped in his tracks and pulled a cellular phone out of his pocket. "I'm calling security," he said tersely.

"Who do you suppose she is?" George asked Nancy.

"I don't know, but I plan to find out," Nancy said firmly. She hurried to the exit door and flung

11

it open. On the other side was a dimly lit stairway—and no sign of the woman. Nancy listened intently, trying to hear the woman's footsteps. But all she heard was silence.

Nancy frowned. "I wonder where she went?"

"She could have gone either upstairs or down— I'll check it out," George volunteered.

Nancy started down the stairs. "Okay. Ask anyone you run into if they saw a woman fitting her description."

"Got it," George replied.

As she made her way down the stairs, Nancy kept her eyes open for clues; it was possible that the woman had dropped something that might reveal her identity. But Nancy found nothing.

Eventually she reached the lobby level. Exiting the stairwell, Nancy was heading over to ask the clerk if he'd seen the woman in the red sunglasses when the elevator opened. Mr. Lambert stepped out.

Nancy rushed up to him. "Any luck?"

Mr. Lambert shook his head. "I've got security working on it. So far, they haven't located her." He added, "Of course, there may be a simple explanation for all this. She could be a guest here—perhaps she found herself on the wrong floor."

"Wouldn't you have recognized her if she were a guest?" Nancy pointed out.

"With those sunglasses, no," Mr. Lambert replied. "Besides, we have over two hundred suites, and right now we're filled almost to capacity. There's no way I could remember all those faces."

Nancy thought for a moment. "Who has keys to my father's suite?"

"Mr. Drew and I—that's all," Mr. Lambert said.

"The maids have master keys, though, right?" Nancy asked him.

"Well, of course. But I'm sure they're all accounted for." Mr. Lambert frowned. "Perhaps I should talk to Housekeeping, just to be sure." He handed Nancy the key to Suite 312. "Why don't you start looking through your father's suite? I'll join you there in a minute."

"Sounds like a good plan," Nancy said.

Nancy returned to Suite 312. Before going in, she pressed her ear against the door. There were no sounds coming from inside. She also checked the lock—it was possible that the woman had already broken in before Nancy and the others had surprised her. But there were no scratches around the keyhole.

"Okay, here goes," Nancy said to herself. She put the key in the lock and opened the door, then flicked the light switch on.

Just then she heard a noise behind her. She spun around.

It was George. "Sorry if I scared you," she said sheepishly. "Did you find her?"

Nancy relaxed and shook her head. "No, you?"

"Nope," George replied. "I went up and down all the floors from four to ten. It's a good thing I've been hitting the stair-climbing machine at the gym. That was a lot of steps!"

The girls went into the suite. It consisted of a living room, bedroom, and bathroom, decorated simply but elegantly in beige and brown tones. Doing a quick, superficial search, Nancy didn't notice anything out of place—or obviously missing. If the woman had broken in, she hadn't turned the furniture upside down or rooted through the dresser drawers in a mad frenzy.

Pausing in the bedroom, Nancy opened the closet door. Inside was one suit, several shirts and ties, as well as a pair of brown leather shoes. The clothes still smelled faintly of her father's aftershave. Nancy inhaled the familiar scent and was overwhelmed with sadness.

"This is so weird," she said softly to George. "I mean, here's all his stuff, and yet he's . . ."

George put a hand on Nancy's shoulder. "I know. If it were my father, I'd feel the same way."

Nancy took a deep breath. She had to stick to business—she had to find her father!

Standing on her toes, Nancy peered at the top shelf of the closet. There sat her father's tan suitcase. She recalled that it was the only luggage he'd had with him when she drove him to the airport last Sunday. "It's pretty clear that he didn't go on a side trip somewhere," she said to

George, pointing to the suitcase. "Or, if he did, he didn't pack anything."

"What do you suppose that means?" George asked.

"I'm not sure," Nancy replied slowly. "Listen, let's split up and do an in-depth search. You take the living room, and I'll keep working in here. Look for any clues to his whereabouts: addresses, phone numbers, a letter, a plane ticket . . . things like that."

After George left for the living room, Nancy continued her search of the bedroom. There was nothing in the pockets of her dad's clothes except some change and an old dry cleaner's tag. She found nothing of interest in his dresser drawers, either. The bed had been made—no doubt on Tuesday morning by one of the maids. On the pillow was a chocolate-covered mint wrapped in green foil.

Then Nancy noticed something on his night-stand: a dog-eared edition of Shakespeare's plays.

Sitting down on the edge of the bed, she picked up the book and flipped through its pages. She remembered that the week before, back in River Heights, her father had been in the middle of *King Lear*. It had been his favorite play in college, he'd told her.

She found a bookmark slipped in the middle of a different play: *Macbeth*. Except that it wasn't just a bookmark. It was a piece of lined notebook paper with a list of names.

Nancy pulled it out and studied it with curiosity. The names were in blue ink, in her father's familiar handwriting:

MAKE APPTS W/
LYMAN TREMAIN
PAGE DURRELL
GABRIELLA CIARDI
ARISTOTLE KIRIAKIS
JULIAN ST. JAMES

At the bottom of the list was a sketchy drawing of a falcon, also in blue ink. Its wings were folded, and its head was turned to the left.

Nancy frowned. Who were these people? she wondered. Were they part of a case her father was working on or five separate, unrelated appointments he planned to make? And what was the meaning of the falcon drawing?

George entered the room and plopped down on the bed next to Nancy. "Did you find something?"

Nancy showed her the list. George scanned it quickly, then said, "Do you think it's a clue?"

"Possibly," Nancy said thoughtfully. "If these people are in New York, and Dad made appointments to see them this week, one of them might know where he is." She added, "But this falcon drawing has me stumped. What could it possibly mean?"

* * *

16

Bess put her chopsticks down abruptly and began waving her hand in front of her mouth. "This stuff is hot!" she exclaimed in surprise.

Nancy's aunt chuckled and handed Bess a dish of rice. "Here, have some of this," she said. "It's the best cure I know for chili-pepper chicken overdose." Bess nodded gratefully and gulped some down.

Eloise Drew, Bess, Nancy, and George were having dinner in a Thai restaurant. A small, intimate place with a dozen tables, it was packed, and there was a line going out the door. The air was filled with delicious, exotic smells.

Nancy took a bite of *pad thai*—noodles with shrimp, vegetables, and crumbled peanuts—and turned to her aunt. "So you guys didn't have any luck this afternoon, huh?"

Aunt Eloise shook her head. "Your father didn't leave Manhattan anytime in the last few days by plane, train, bus, or rental car," she reported. "Unless he went by train or bus without a reservation and paid in cash."

Nancy looked thoughtful. "It's still hard to believe that Dad would have left town without telling anyone," she mused. "Plus, there's the fact that his only suitcase is still in his hotel suite."

George elbowed her. "Show them the list, Nan."

"List? What list?" Bess asked curiously.

Nancy fished it out of her purse and handed it to

her aunt and Bess. "I found this in a book on Dad's nightstand," she explained.

As Bess scanned it, her eyes opened wide. "Your dad knows Gabriella Ciardi? That's so cool!" She exclaimed.

Nancy was startled. "You know who she is?"

"Only the editor in chief of my favorite magazine, *Bellissima*," Bess said eagerly. "She always writes a little column in the front of every issue— 'Greetings from Gabriella.'"

Aunt Eloise read the list over Bess's shoulder. "I don't know Gabriella Ciardi, but I recognize some of these other names," she murmured. "Page Durrell is the curator of the New York Museum of Art. I know because I just got a mailing from her, asking for money for the museum. Julian St. James is a big Broadway director—I read somewhere that he's got a new play coming out soon. As for Lyman Tremain . . ."

She paused and began rooting through her oversize leather purse. She fished out the Metro section of that day's paper. "Yes, here we go— here's an article about Lyman Tremain. He's a judge, and he's running for state attorney general in the fall."

"What about Aristotle Kiriakis?" Nancy asked.

Aunt Eloise frowned. "His name doesn't ring a bell, but he may be in the phone book."

Nancy's mind was racing. It seemed safe to assume that her father planned to make appointments with all five people during his stay in New

18

York. But why not have Ms. Hanson call them? She didn't think they were personal friends of her dad—she'd never heard him mention any of their names. Perhaps he'd decided to meet with them only after arriving in New York and figured it would be easier to call them directly rather than go through Ms. Hanson.

Then she remembered the falcon drawing and pointed it out to her aunt. "Does this mean anything to you?"

Aunt Eloise shrugged. "Maybe your father was just doodling."

"What about that woman you saw?" Bess spoke up. She had finished her chili-pepper chicken and had moved on to a dish of beef curry. "Did the manager call the police or anything?"

"No," Nancy replied. "Mr. Lambert didn't want to call the police. Nothing seemed to be gone from Dad's suite, and there was no sign of a break-in. He checked with the maids, and none of their master keys was missing. He thinks the woman must have been a guest on the wrong floor or something."

"What do you think, Nan?" Bess asked her.

"Mr. Lambert could be right," Nancy said slowly. "But then, why did she run away from us like that?"

The foursome continued to discuss the case as they finished up their dinner. It was after nine o'clock when they left the restaurant.

It was a warm night, and the street was packed

with pedestrians. On the corner a man was playing a jazzy song on a saxophone.

Aunt Eloise paused at a florist's window to admire the display. Then she turned to the girls. "If anyone still has room for dessert. I've got some ice cream back at the apartment," she announced cheerfully. "There's a carton of chocolate macadamia nut and half a carton of—" Her voice broke off.

Nancy tensed up. "What is it, Aunt Eloise?"

Eloise pointed a shaky finger at a bus that was halfway down the block. A middle-aged man was just getting on it. "There he is!" she cried out. "There's Carson!"

3

Tailed by a Stranger

Nancy gazed intently at the man. He does look like Dad, she thought eagerly.

Without wasting another second, Nancy took off down the sidewalk. The bus doors were just closing, and she could hear the driver shifting gears. "Stop!" she shouted, just ten feet away from the bus. "*Stop!*" she shouted again, louder. Out of the corner of her eye, she noticed people pausing on the sidewalk to stare at her.

Summoning all her energy, Nancy put on an extra burst of speed and managed to catch up to the front of the bus. Running alongside it, she banged frantically on the door. "Stop! Let me on!"

The bus stopped, and the door swung open. The driver glowered down at her. "I've got a schedule to keep," he said curtly.

"Thank you," Nancy said breathlessly. She leaped up the stairs and glanced around the crowded bus. None of the passengers seemed interested in her, except a few who looked annoyed by the delay.

"Hey, miss!" the driver barked. "You gonna pay your fare? Exact change or a token."

Nancy began digging through her purse, all the while scanning the bus for her father's face.

Then she saw his back a few feet away. She pushed through the crowd in the aisle and put her hand on his arm. "Dad!" she exclaimed happily.

The man turned around—and Nancy felt a wave of disappointment wash over her. His height, build, and coloring were similar—but he wasn't Carson Drew.

"Oh—I'm sorry," Nancy said, blushing. "I thought you were someone else."

Nancy took a sip of her coffee, then sat back on the couch and prepared to make another phone call. The morning sun streamed through the windows, and classical music was playing softly on the radio. Her aunt was puttering in the kitchen; Bess and George were still at the dining-room table, finishing their breakfasts and reading the paper.

George glanced up from the sports section. "So, who have you called so far?" she asked Nancy.

"Just Ms. Hanson," Nancy replied. "I asked her about the five names on the list—she says she doesn't know anything about them. They're no

ven in Dad's address file. The falcon drawing
oesn't mean anything to her, either." She added,
I'm going to try calling these five people myself
nd see if they'll give me appointments."

"How will you find their phone numbers?" Bess
asked her.

Nancy scanned her father's list. "I can call
Gabriella Ciardi at *Bellissima*, and Page Durrell at
the New York Museum of Art. Lyman Tremain is a
judge, so I can probably call some general information number down at City Hall. As for Julian St.
James—Aunt Eloise mentioned that he's in rehearsal with a new play. I wonder which theater
it's in?"

Aunt Eloise popped her head out of the kitchen,
wiping her hands on a towel. "I can ask my
neighbor across the hall. He's a theater fanatic—
he'll know." She put the towel down and headed
for the front door. "I'll stop by there right now."

"Great," Nancy said. "In the meantime, we still
have to find out who Aristotle Kiriakis is. He's not
listed in the Manhattan phone book."

Nancy took another sip of coffee, then dialed
the number for *Bellissima.* She asked the receptionist to put her through to Gabriella Ciardi.

After what seemed like a hundred rings, someone picked up the phone. "Where *is* that stupid
secretary of mine?" a woman muttered, then:
"Yes? Hello?"

"Hi," Nancy said quickly. "I'd like to speak to
Gabriella Ciardi."

23

"Speaking," the woman said impatiently.

"My name is Nancy Drew," Nancy said. "I'm calling about my father, Carson Drew. I believe he made an appointment to see you this week. He disappeared, and I'm trying to—"

"Listen, Miss whatever your name is," Ms. Ciardi cut in crisply. "I'm the editor in chief of this magazine. Editor in chief, do you understand? I don't have time for things like this. If you're having problems keeping track of your father, buy a beeper." Then she hung up abruptly.

Nancy frowned. "Great. I guess I'd better try her again later, when she's in a better mood." Then she dialed the number for the New York Museum of Art. "Hello?" she said to the receptionist. "Page Durrell, please."

Several moments later a man's voice replied, "This is Page Durrell's office. Can I help you?"

After Nancy explained what she wanted, the secretary said, "Carson Drew? His name sounds familiar to me—I believe he called here earlier this week. But Ms. Durrell makes her own appointments, so I can't tell you for sure if she saw him. Let me ask her—hang on just a second."

Nancy felt a surge of optimism. If her father had met with Page Durrell, then the museum curator might have some information about him.

But her hopes were dashed when the secretary came back on the line. "I'm sorry," he said, "but Ms. Durrell says her appointments are strictly confidential."

"But—" Nancy protested.

"I'm sorry we couldn't help," the secretary went on. "Have a nice day." Then he hung up.

"No luck?" George called out.

"No," Nancy replied with a sigh. "But I have a few more people to try."

The front door opened just then, and Eloise walked in. "My neighbor says that Julian St. James is at the Gotham Theater," she announced.

"Thanks!" Nancy picked up the phone book and found a listing for the Gotham. She dialed the number.

A voice with an English accent answered. "Hello?"

"Julian St. James, please," Nancy said.

"This is he."

"My name is Nancy Drew, and I—"

"—want a part in *Deadly Secrets*, right? You and a thousand other people. Have your agent contact me." Then the director hung up.

Nancy stared in amazement at the phone. "What's with these people, anyway?"

"They're all celebrities," Bess replied, taking a bite of her blueberry muffin. "People like that don't have time to talk to mere mortals like us."

Fortunately, Nancy had better luck with Lyman Tremain, whom she found after making several calls. His clerk, Rosemary, told her that he would meet with her in his chambers at eleven. "The judge says he did speak to your father earlier this week, and he'll be glad to talk to you about it,"

25

Rosemary said to Nancy. "Do you know how to get down here?"

"I think so," Nancy replied. Just then she recalled something Miguel Lopez had told her: that her father had asked for directions to the City Hall area on Monday afternoon. Could he have been going to meet with Lyman Tremain? It would make sense, since Carson was a lawyer and Lyman Tremain was a judge.

While Aunt Eloise went off to the library to track down Aristotle Kiriakis, Nancy, George, and Bess took a subway down to the City Hall area. Judge Tremain's chambers were in a beautiful old marble courthouse overlooking a small park.

Rosemary, his clerk, greeted the girls. "He's expecting you," she told them. "I should warn you, though—he's got only a few minutes until his next appointment."

Judge Tremain rose from his desk when the girls walked in. He was tall and slender, with dark hair that was graying at the temples. "Hi—Sonny Tremain," he said in a deep, warm voice.

Bess looked confused. "Sonny? I thought your name was Lyman."

"It's a nickname I've had since childhood," the judge explained, smiling. "Please—have a seat."

Nancy glanced around. The wall behind the judge's desk was covered with diplomas and family photos, and the other walls were lined with books. A large American flag stood in one corner.

Turning her attention back to the judge, Nancy

introduced herself and her friends. "I'm Carson Drew's daughter," she went on. "He came to New York on business, but he seems to have disappeared. I thought you might be able to help me."

"I wish I could." Judge Tremain folded his hands and leaned back in his chair. "Your father called me early Monday morning and asked me for an appointment. He explained that he was a lawyer and had to see me about some legal business. I told him he could come by that afternoon at three."

So Dad was heading down to this area after his lunch meeting with Miguel Lopez, Nancy thought. Out loud, she said, "What happened at your meeting?"

"Nothing," the judge replied. "He never arrived, and he didn't call to cancel. I never heard from him again."

George frowned. "That doesn't sound like your dad, Nan."

"It sure doesn't," Nancy said. It didn't make sense, she thought. Her father had spent Monday night at his hotel, and Ms. Hanson had talked to him on the phone Tuesday morning. So why hadn't he shown up for his appointment on Monday with the judge?

Nancy turned to Judge Tremain. "Do you have any idea why he wanted to see you?"

The judge shrugged. "I didn't press for details. He was a fellow member of the bar, so I spared him a few minutes. Although I must admit that I was a little annoyed when he didn't show up." He added, "I'm curious—how did you know he wanted to see me?"

Nancy dug the list of names out of her purse and showed it to him. "I found this in his hotel suite last night. In fact, maybe you could help me: Do you know who Aristotle Kiriakis is?"

Judge Tremain reached into the pocket of his jacket and pulled out a pair of silver, wire-rimmed glasses. He put them on and peered at the list. "Aristotle Kiriakis. Doesn't ring a bell. Neither do these other names, for that matter." He chuckled. "My wife will be the first to tell you, though—I'm terrible with names. After twenty years of marriage, I still can't keep her side of the family straight."

"How about the drawing of the falcon?" Nancy persisted. "Does that mean anything to you?"

The judge glanced at it. "No. Why—should it?"

Rosemary's voice rang out over the intercom. "Your next appointment is here, Judge Tremain."

"Thank you, Rosemary. Ask him to wait just a second." The judge rose to his feet. "I assume you've filed a missing persons report, Nancy. Why don't I give the police a call and get them to put the search for your dad on the front burner?" He placed a hand on Nancy's shoulder and smiled sympathetically. "I have a daughter your age, and I know how she'd feel if something happened to me."

"That's very kind of you—thank you," Nancy told him gratefully. "And if the police give you any information, here's where I can be reached." She wrote her aunt's phone number on a piece of paper and handed it to the judge.

As the girls left the courthouse, Bess said, "Well, he was nice."

"He sure was—especially compared to Gabriella Ciardi, Julian St. James, and Page Durrell." Nancy added, "I wonder why Dad never made it to his meeting with him?"

"Your guess is as good as mine," George replied.

Just then some instinct told Nancy that she was being watched. She turned around and noticed a man staring at her and her friends. He had tousled gray hair, dark beady eyes, and pockmarked skin. Leaning idly against a streetlight, in a brown suit, he looked out of place among the straitlaced lawyers and government officials.

"Nan?" Bess tugged on her sleeve. "Where to now?"

Nancy turned and tried to focus on Bess's question. The gray-haired man gave her the creeps.

"We're pretty close to Chinatown," Nancy said. "Why don't we walk over there, have an early lunch, then call Aunt Eloise for a progress report?"

"Sounds great," George said, and Bess nodded enthusiastically.

Twenty minutes later the three girls were walking down Canal Street in Chinatown. They gazed in fascination at the roast ducks hanging in the store windows, the vegetable stands overflowing with exotic-looking produce, and the seafood markets with their outdoor displays of glassy-eyed fish, eels, and squid. The sidewalks were jammed with shoppers, most of whom were speaking in rapid-fire Chinese.

"This is so much fun!" Bess said loudly, trying to be heard above the chaos. "Where should we eat? There's about a million restaurants to choose from."

"There's a good place around here somewhere," Nancy said, glancing across the street. "I went there once with Dad and Aunt Eloise—" Then something caught her eye.

It was the gray-haired man who'd been staring at them in front of the courthouse. He was standing on the sidewalk on the other side of Canal Street, peering at them over the top of his newspaper. When he noticed Nancy looking at him, he wheeled around and slipped through the crowd of people on the sidewalk. He disappeared into a nearby alley.

Nancy felt a chill go down her spine. The man seemed to be following them. But why?

4

An Unexpected Clue

George put a hand on Nancy's elbow. "What is it, Nan? Did you see someone you recognize?"

Nancy started across the street. "Come this way. I think there's a guy following us."

Bess rushed after Nancy. "But why would someone follow *us*?"

"I'm not sure," Nancy replied tersely. "But I plan to find out."

She crossed the street and hurried over to the alley. Sandwiched between two rows of apartment buildings, it was narrow and dark. The gray-haired man was nowhere in sight; all Nancy could see were Dumpsters overflowing with garbage and pigeons nesting on the windowsills.

"I wonder where he went?" she said to George and Bess, who were right behind her.

"What made you think this guy was following us?" Bess asked Nancy.

"I noticed him staring at us outside Judge Tremain's courthouse," Nancy said, "and then I saw him again watching us from this side of the street."

"This is really weird," George remarked. "Yesterday, there was that woman with the red sunglasses outside your dad's hotel suite. Now there may or may not be some guy following us. Do you think either one of them might be connected to your dad's disappearance?"

Nancy was silent as she considered this. It was totally possible, she realized. And if the woman with the red sunglasses or the gray-haired man were involved, it might mean that her father was in trouble—maybe even the victim of foul play!

Oh, Dad, Nancy thought despondently. Where are you? Are you okay?

Nancy and her friends circled the block twice in search of the gray-haired man, but there was no sign of him. Finally they decided to give up and have some lunch.

An hour later, stomachs full of hot and sour soup and vegetable lo mein, the three girls walked out into the sunshine. Nancy headed for one of the distinctive Chinatown public phones, shaped like a Chinese pagoda. "I want to call Aunt Eloise and get an update," she told the others. "Maybe she has some good news."

Bess pointed in the opposite direction. "I'll just be over at that stand checking out those cute little silk slippers. George, you want to come with me?"

"Oh, I guess," George grumbled.

Nancy got her aunt on the second ring. "Hi, it's me. Any luck?"

"Yes and no," Eloise Drew said. "Gabriella Ciardi called a short while ago. She said she's had a change of heart, and she can see you at the *Bellissima* office at two-thirty. Then, right after that, Julian St. James called. He said he'll give you ten minutes at four o'clock."

"That's great," Nancy said eagerly. She was somewhat surprised that they'd decided to grant her appointments after being so rude to her. Still, she wasn't going to question her turn of luck. "How about Page Durrell?"

"I haven't heard from her," Aunt Eloise replied. "By the way, I spent some time at the library trying to find Aristotle Kiriakis. I checked the phone books for Long Island, Brooklyn, and Queens—plus anywhere in Connecticut and New Jersey within a hundred-mile radius. He's not listed."

"I have an idea," Nancy said. "Why don't you call the other Kiriakises listed in the phone books and ask for him? It's kind of a long shot, but you might get one of his relatives." She added, "If you do, you'll have to make up a good story as to why you want Aristotle Kiriakis's number."

"I can handle it," Eloise said, chuckling. "After all, I'm not a famous detective's aunt for nothing!"

Bellissima's offices were in a converted warehouse in the heart of SoHo, a trendy neighborhood full of art galleries, boutiques, and restaurants. The reception area was decorated entirely in white: white leather couches, white coffee tables, and enormous vases of white tulips. On the white walls were framed blow-ups of the magazine's past covers. Rock music was playing over invisible speakers.

"Somebody pinch me," Bess said, looking around with awe. "I can't believe we're here."

Nancy headed up to the receptionist, who was sitting behind a clear Lucite desk talking on the phone. The woman pushed the Hold button and glanced up. "Yes?"

Nancy introduced herself. "I have an appointment to see Gabriella Ciardi at two-thirty."

"Hang on." The woman dialed a number and spoke into the phone briefly. After a moment a slim young woman with spiky red hair appeared through a set of double doors. She was dressed in a black miniskirt, oversize white T-shirt, and thigh-high red boots.

She smiled at Nancy. "Hi. You're the new paste-up artist, right?"

Nancy was taken aback. "Um, no. I'm Nancy Drew," she said. "These are my friends George

34

Fayne and Bess Marvin. We have an appointment with Ms. Ciardi."

"Oh." The young woman looked confused. Then she threw up her hands. "Oh, well, whatever—I'm all mixed up. Come on back. By the way, I'm Cassie Dake, Ms. Ciardi's assistant."

The girls followed Cassie through a set of double doors. On the other side was a huge loft space with floor-to-ceiling windows overlooking SoHo. Individual offices were partitioned off by glass block walls. Dozens of people were furiously typing away on computers.

"Wouldn't it be cool if I could work here someday?" Bess whispered to Nancy.

Cassie turned around. "You want to work *here?*" she said in amazement. "But why?"

Bess blushed deeply. "Well, er, because *Bellissima* is my favorite magazine," she said.

"If you love the magazine, stick to reading it," Cassie said in a low voice. "Working on it is a whole different thing. The deadlines are totally insane, the hours are long, and the people are crabby, if you know what I mean." She stopped short. "Oops, enough gossip. Here we are."

Cassie paused in front of an open doorway. Inside was an enormous corner office with deep violet walls, a red leather couch, and an eclectic mix of Art Deco furniture. Vases of red roses were everywhere, filling the air with a sweet, heady fragrance.

A woman of about forty rose from behind a huge black-and-chrome desk. A wild tumble of black, shoulder-length curls framed her slim, pointy face. Her perfectly tailored red suit made her look as chic as any model on the *Bellissima* covers, Nancy thought.

"Gabriella Ciardi," the woman said briskly. She fixed her large green eyes on Cassie. "You can go, Cass. Remember, I need a hundred copies of that skin cream article by four o'clock. And don't forget to reschedule my pedicure and hypnosis appointments."

"Whoops—I thought you said to reschedule your manicure and aromatherapy appointments." Cassie flew out of the office. "Don't worry, Ms. Ciardi—I'll take care of it."

When she'd gone, Ms. Ciardi shook her head. "That girl is so incompetent," she said. "I'd fire her in a second if I had the time to break in a new assistant." She returned to her seat. "Now, which one of you is Nancy Drew?"

"That's me." Nancy sat down on the red leather couch, and Bess and George followed suit. "These are my friends Bess Marvin and George Fayne."

"I'm a huge fan of your magazine," Bess gushed.

"How very nice," Ms. Ciardi said coolly. She picked a piece of paper off her desk, glanced at it distractedly, then let it flutter back down. "Now, Ms. Drew, you mentioned that your father is missing. Well, what can I say? He called on

Monday asking to meet with me. That brainless secretary of mine automatically gave him the appointment without asking him what it was about—just because he identified himself as a lawyer." She added, "The appointment was for Tuesday at nine A.M., but he never showed up."

Nancy frowned. "Why not?"

"I have no idea—he never called to cancel. And that was the last I heard of him." Ms. Ciardi brushed an invisible piece of lint off her suit. "I must say, I found your father's behavior a tad *rude*. I'm a very busy woman."

Nancy was silent. The exact same thing had happened Monday afternoon with Judge Tremain. It wasn't like her father to make appointments, then break them without even bothering to call.

And the sequence of events didn't make sense. Her father had kept his Monday lunch date with Miguel Lopez but missed his Monday afternoon meeting with the judge. He'd spent Monday night at his hotel, and called Ms. Hanson Tuesday morning, but he never showed for his Tuesday morning meeting with Gabriella Ciardi.

What was going on? Nancy wondered.

The telephone rang. Ms. Ciardi glared at it, then picked it up. "Yes? What is it, Roger?" She listened for a minute, then barked, "Tell the little prima donna that I won't listen to any more whiny excuses about missing her deadline. If she doesn't get that piece in by tomorrow morning, she can kiss her fee goodbye. Got it?" She slammed down

37

the phone and smiled tightly at Nancy and her friends. "Now, where were we?"

Nancy took the list she'd found in her father's suite out of her purse. She crossed the room to show it to Ms. Ciardi. "Do you know any of these other people?" she asked. "Especially Aristotle Kiriakis?"

Ms. Ciardi peered at the list. "I've heard of Julian St. James and Judge Tremain, of course, but I don't know them personally," she said. "As for Page Durrell, the magazine interviewed her a while back, and I believe I met her at the photo shoot." She handed the list back to Nancy. "I have no idea who this Aristotle person is."

"What about the falcon?" Nancy asked, pointing to the sketch. "Does that mean anything to you?"

Ms. Ciardi put her fingers on her temples and closed her eyes. "What is this, a quiz? Isn't it the national bird of Canada or something?"

The phone rang again. Ms. Ciardi opened her eyes and picked it up. "Yes? What? What do you *mean* he can't do the layout by Monday? Tell him that if he doesn't, I'll make sure he never works in this town again." She covered the mouthpiece with her hand and said, "If there's nothing else, Ms. Drew, I have a little emergency to attend to."

Nancy put the list back in her purse. "No," she said, "there's nothing else. Thank you for your time. If I have any more questions, I'll give you a call."

38

As she, George, and Bess slipped out of the office, they could hear the editor in chief screaming at the person on the other end of the phone. "She must be a blast to work for," George said dryly.

"Speaking of which . . ." Nancy spotted Cassie sitting at her desk, filing her nails. "Hey, Cassie? Could I ask you a few questions?" she called out.

Cassie turned around. "Oh, sure. What, you want to know our models' beauty secrets or something?"

"Yes!" Bess said eagerly.

"No," Nancy said at the same time. "Listen, Cassie, my father, Carson Drew, called here on Monday to make an appointment with Ms. Ciardi. You gave him one for nine o'clock on Tuesday. Do you remember?"

"Carson Drew. Carson Drew." Cassie shook her head. "I'm not sure. I make so *many* appointments for her, you know?" Then her face lit up. "Oh, now it's coming back to me. He's the director of *Teenage Vampires from Biloxi,* right?"

Nancy smiled. "Um, no. He's a lawyer."

"Oh." Cassie shrugged. "Sorry, his name just doesn't ring a bell." She added, "Hey, you guys want to come to a *Bellissima* party tomorrow night? It's a big spring fashion issue blowout."

"Are you kidding?" Bess said immediately. "We'd love to come."

"I just have to find you some passes." Cassie opened her desk drawer and began rooting through it. She pulled out several dogeared paperbacks, a pair of pantyhose, and a stack of bright pink phone message slips. "They've *got* to be here somewhere."

Nancy glanced casually at the growing pile on Cassie's desk—and did a double take.

One of the phone messages had yesterday's date and said: "Cassie: Call Miguel Lopez ASAP."

Nancy's mind began racing. Was this Miguel Lopez the lawyer—the one her father had met with on Monday? If Cassie knew him, did she know more about Carson Drew than she was letting on?

5

The Blue Handkerchief

Nancy stared at Cassie, who was still rooting through her desk and chatting animatedly about its contents. She seemed so sweet—and yet Nancy knew all too well that appearances could be deceiving. Whatever her connection to Miguel Lopez was, Nancy just had to find out.

"Hey, Cassie?" Nancy said, trying to sound casual. "I couldn't help but notice. How do you happen to know—"

At that moment Gabriella Ciardi poked her head out her office door. "Cassie, get in here right away. I need you to take a memo." She frowned at Nancy and her friends, then went back into her office.

"Coming, Ms. Ciardi. Hey, here they are!" Cassie produced a pile of yellow passes from underneath a half-eaten sandwich. She handed four of them to Nancy. "Take an extra—you can bring a friend. Listen, I've got to go." She gave the girls a quick smile, then rushed into Ms. Ciardi's office.

Nancy waited for a second, then glanced around. There were no other *Bellissima* employees nearby. She moved closer to Cassie's desk and started leafing surreptitiously through her other phone messages.

"Nancy—what are you doing?" George whispered in disbelief.

"Later, okay?" Nancy whispered back.

A young guy was coming down the corridor, carrying an armload of files. He stared suspiciously at Nancy as she flicked through Cassie's papers. "Can I help you with something?" he asked.

Nancy looked up and smiled sweetly at him. She swiftly tried to think of a good reason why she was searching through Cassie's desk. "I, uh, was just looking for a pen so I could leave a note for Cassie," she stammered. That was actually the truth—she *did* want to arrange to talk to Cassie about Miguel Lopez.

The guy reached into his pocket and found a ballpoint pen. "Here, try this."

"Great." Nancy bent down, ripped a page from a legal pad, and wrote: "Cassie: Please call me. Nancy Drew." She added her aunt Eloise's number, then returned the pen to the young man. "Thanks a lot."

"You're welcome," he grunted. Hefting his armload of files, he disappeared down the hallway.

Nancy wanted to continue her search, but she didn't want to take any chances that he'd come back. "Come on, girls, let's go," she said to George and Bess.

"But—" George began.

"I'll explain outside," Nancy said firmly.

Out on the sidewalk Bess put her hands on her hips and said, "Okay, Nan—what was that all about?"

Nancy told her friends about the Miguel Lopez phone message. "It's kind of a weird coincidence that Cassie and Mr. Lopez know each other, don't you think?" she finished.

"There's no way Cassie had anything to do with your father's disappearance, though," Bess protested. "She's so nice!"

"Still, I think we should check out this lead," Nancy insisted. "And while we're waiting for Cassie to call us, I'm going to call Mr. Lopez." Nancy headed over to a phone booth on the corner, inserted a quarter, then dialed his number.

After several rings a voice answered: "Good afternoon—Sanborne, Lopez, and Chang."

"I'd like to speak to Miguel Lopez," she said. "This is Nancy Drew."

"I'm sorry, Ms. Drew," the secretary said. "Mr.

Lopez is out of town until Monday. Can I take a message?"

Nancy frowned. "No, no message—I'll try him again next week."

"No luck?" George asked her when she'd hung up.

"He's out of town," Nancy explained, then glanced around. "Hey, where's Bess?"

"Where else?" George nodded toward a shop window displaying earrings made of plastic dolls' heads. Bess was peering through the glass.

As they walked over to join her, George said, "So, you're really adding Cassie to your suspect list?"

"For now," Nancy replied. "So far, we've got the woman with the red sunglasses, the gray-haired guy who was tailing us in Chinatown, Miguel Lopez, and Cassie. None of them are very strong suspects, though, and we're not any closer to finding Dad." She sighed. "I hope we have better luck when we meet with Julian St. James."

The Gotham Theater was located in midtown, in the theater district. As they walked through the neighborhood, Nancy, George, and Bess passed one theater after another, all with brightly colored marquees advertising their shows.

Nancy stopped in front of an old, elegant gray building. "The Gotham—here it is."

"I can't believe we're going to meet a real Broadway director," Bess said eagerly as they

44

went inside. She was wearing the plastic doll's-head earrings that she'd bought in SoHo. "I wonder what he'll be like?"

"If he's anything like he was on the phone, he won't be incredibly polite," Nancy said wryly.

Inside the building Nancy went up to the box office and told the woman inside that she had an appointment with Julian St. James. The woman directed the three girls into the auditorium.

There, rehearsal was in progress. Nancy, George, and Bess hovered in the back and stared in fascination. The stage had been transformed into a Victorian-style parlor, with dark green velvet couches, ornately carved furniture, burgundy-colored walls, and a grandfather clock. In the background was a beautiful stained-glass window as well as a staircase leading to an offstage second floor.

On one of the couches sat two young men. "So you're saying you haven't seen Monica lately?" one of them said in a loud, dramatic voice.

"No," the other one replied. "Not since Christmas, at least." He raised his eyebrows. "Why? Have *you*?"

A middle-aged man appeared out of the wings, clapping his hands. He was short and slender, with a long blond ponytail and wearing a black turtleneck and black pants. "Take that again, please," he called out in a cultured-sounding English accent. "Tony, try to remember: You *want* Spencer McTavish to know that you're lying about

45

Monica. You're playing a game with him, manipulating him."

One of the actors nodded. "Right, Julian."

"Enjoying the show?"

Nancy whirled around. A tall, husky young guy with light brown skin and dreadlocks was standing behind them. He was dressed in faded jeans and a black T-shirt.

"We're waiting for Mr. St. James," Nancy explained, nodding toward the blond man on the stage. "We have an appointment with him."

"That's cool." He smiled, and his smile seemed to gravitate naturally toward Bess. "And what's your name?" he asked her.

"Bess Marvin," she said, smiling back at him. Watching Bess in action, Nancy couldn't help but grin. Her friend was a natural flirt.

"I'm Quito Messenger," the guy said. "So, like I was asking—how are you enjoying the show?"

"We just got here," George told him. "But it seems great so far."

Quito's brown eyes sparkled merrily. "Good," he said, "because I'm in it. In fact, it's my first Broadway gig."

"You're *in* it?" Bess said excitedly. "Wow, that's so cool! What part do you—?"

"Excuse me! Hello, there!"

Nancy glanced up. From the stage Julian St. James, was peering impatiently out at the seats. Hands on his hips, he stared right at Nancy, Bess, George, and Quito. "I'm sorry, Quito, but you

46

can't be inviting your friends here," he called out. "This is a closed rehearsal."

"We're not with him," Nancy said loudly. "I'm Nancy Drew—I have an appointment to see you at four o'clock."

"Nancy Dr— Oh, yes." The director looked around distractedly for a moment, then announced, "We'll take a ten-minute break. Quito, you and Marcus should go over your lines for Scene Four."

"Right, Julian." Quito smiled at Bess again and started toward the stage. "See you all later."

Julian St. James trotted down to where Nancy and her friends were standing. He fixed his small black eyes on George and Bess. "And who are you two, may I ask?" he said, sounding annoyed.

"These are my friends George Fayne and Bess Marvin," Nancy said quickly.

"I wasn't expecting them, but—oh, very well." He shrugged. "Come back to my office, then."

The director led them to a small room behind the stage area. Its dingy green walls were covered with old theater posters, and its only furnishings were a metal desk, a file cabinet, and several folding chairs.

He sat down behind the desk and clasped his hands together. "As I said to my actors—ten minutes."

Nancy sat down in one of the folding chairs, then showed him the list she'd found in her father's hotel suite. "I'm assuming from this that my father tried to make an appointment with you sometime this week," she began.

Mr. St. James studied the list. "My, your father seems to know some very important people in town," he commented. "Gabriella Ciardi . . . Sonny Tremain . . . Page Durrell . . ."

"You know these people?" Nancy asked him.

"Only by reputation. I'm not acquainted with them personally." Mr. St. James added, "Actually, I've never heard of this Kiriakis fellow."

"So, *did* Nancy's dad come to see you, Mr. St. James?" George spoke up. She was sitting on the chair next to Nancy's, and Bess was seated on the other side of her.

The director put his fingertips together and propped them under his chin. "Let me think," he said. "He rang up on Monday and asked me for an appointment. I gave him one for Tuesday afternoon at three, I believe. But he never made it."

Nancy frowned. Just like with Judge Tremain and Gabriella Ciardi, she thought. "Did he call to cancel?" she asked, although she already knew the answer.

Mr. St. James shook his head. "No. Although I was so involved in rehearsal that day that I hardly noticed his absence."

"Why did he want to see you?" Bess asked him.

"He didn't say. Actually, the whole thing was a peculiar mix-up." The director laughed a nervous little laugh. "When he rang up, I thought that he said he was *Carl* Drew. Carl Drew is one of this

48

show's backers, so naturally I gave him the appointment without hesitation. When I got your call, Ms. Drew, I realized my error: mistaking Carson Drew for Carl Drew.''

Just then Nancy had the instinctive feeling that someone was eavesdropping on their conversation. Ever so casually, she turned in her seat. She caught the shadow of a movement outside the door. The shadow looked like Quito Messenger. What was he doing there? she wondered.

Then Nancy noticed something else. On the linoleum floor under George's chair was a pale blue linen handkerchief embroidered with the letters *CD*. It looked exactly like one she'd given her father the previous Christmas!

Julian St. James has to be lying, Nancy thought. Dad's been here—I just know it!

6

An Artful Ambush

Nancy reached down, picked up the handkerchief, and showed it to Julian St. James. "My father was here, wasn't he?" she demanded.

The director stared at the handkerchief. Nancy wasn't sure, but he seemed to have turned a shade paler. "I—I don't know what you're talking about," he stammered as his eyes trailed over the initials *CD*. "That, uh, belongs to Carl Drew."

"How do you know?" Nancy asked him.

Mr. St. James crossed his arms in front of his chest. "If you must know, Carl Drew was here earlier this afternoon," he declared. "I'm sure that's his handkerchief—because I saw him cleaning his glasses with it. In fact, I'd like it back so I can return it to him."

Nancy regarded the director silently for a moment, then turned her gaze to the handkerchief.

t was made by the same company as the handkerchief she'd given her father; even the initials, *CD*,
were in the same shade of slate blue. It would be
an amazing coincidence if this handkerchief really
did belong to Carl Drew—if there even was such a
person.

Reluctantly she handed Julian St. James the
handkerchief. He grabbed it and stuck it in his
pocket. "Thank you. Now, I'm afraid our ten
minutes are up."

"According to my watch," George began,
"we've got four more—"

"Then your watch must be slow," Mr. St. James
interrupted. "Look, I have a major Broadway
show opening in three weeks. I can't sit around
having idle chats about handkerchiefs and missing
people."

"Just one more thing." Nancy leaned across his
desk and pointed out the falcon drawing to him.
"Does that mean anything to you?"

Mr. St. James snorted. "My, you certainly are
into playing detective, Ms. Drew." He waved his
hand dismissively at the falcon. "Your father was
probably just doodling. Now I must ask you all to
leave."

Without another word the director shuttled the
girls back to the auditorium. When they got there,
he turned and pointed to a door. "That way out,
ladies. It's been a pleasure." His voice was thick
with sarcasm.

"Definitely not a nice guy," George remarked as they headed toward the exit.

"Definitely not," Nancy agreed. "What I want to know is, is he an honest guy? Was he lying about the handkerchief?"

"It would be great if he knew something about your dad, Nan," Bess said hopefully.

Just then Nancy saw Quito Messenger coming down the aisle. Here was her chance to check Julian St. James's story and to find out why Quito had been eavesdropping. "Hey, Quito!" she called out with a smile.

To her surprise, the young actor didn't smile back. In fact, he looked downright uncomfortable. "I'm kind of in a hurry," he said abruptly.

"This will just take a second," Nancy persisted, putting her hand on his arm. "Do you know a man named Carl Drew? He's supposed to be one of the show's backers. Was he around here this afternoon?"

Quito frowned at her. "Listen, I've got to get onstage—my scene's coming up. Excuse me." Then he shrugged off Nancy's hand and went down the aisle.

"Well, that wasn't very helpful," Bess murmured. "I guess he doesn't like me anymore."

"I guess he doesn't like *any* of us anymore," Nancy mused, staring after him thoughtfully. "I wonder what's up?"

*   *   *

"You've got a whipped cream mustache, Bess,"
George told her cousin.

Nancy, George, and Bess were sitting in a café
across the street from the Gotham Theater. Nancy
had suggested an ice-cream soda break to discuss
the case.

"Whoops." Bess dabbed at her lips with a
napkin. Then she glanced at Nancy, who was
scribbling furiously on a piece of paper. "What
are you doing?"

Nancy showed her friends the paper. "I'm trying to reconstruct Dad's schedule. I thought it
would help us out."

The list read:

SUNDAY
Evening: Dad came to NYC. Spent night at
Imperial Hotel.

MONDAY
1 P.M.: Had lunch with Miguel Lopez, lawyer.
May have headed down to City Hall area after-
ward.
3 P.M.: Appointment with Sonny Tremain, judge.
Didn't show up.
Evening: Spent night at Imperial Hotel.

TUESDAY
9 A.M.: Had appointment with Gabriella Ciardi,
editor in chief of *Bellissima.* Didn't show up.
3 P.M.: Had appointment with Julian St. James,
Broadway director. Didn't show up.

5 P.M.: Supposed to send Lopez some important documents by now but didn't.

Evening: Didn't sleep at hotel. Faxes and messages piling up since earlier that day.

WEDNESDAY
7 P.M.: Dinner date with Aunt Eloise. Didn't show up.

George studied the list. "It's so weird," she mused. "He missed his appointment with Judge Tremain, but he showed up at his hotel that night. And he spoke to Ms. Hanson Tuesday morning, right, Nan?"

"Yes, but then he missed his Tuesday appointments." Nancy frowned. "What's the connection between Judge Tremain, Gabriella Ciardi, and Julian St. James?"

George took a sip of her root beer float. "So how's your suspect list shaping up, Nan?"

"Well, we've still got Miguel Lopez, Cassie, the woman with the red sunglasses, and the gray-haired man we saw in Chinatown," Nancy replied. "Plus, there's Julian St. James and Quito Messenger."

"Quito!" Bess exclaimed, looking distressed. "Why Quito? He's such a hunk."

Nancy chuckled. "You know that hunks can be bad guys, too, Bess. And I think Quito was eavesdropping on our conversation with Mr. St. James."

"Maybe Quito was just waiting to talk to him or something," Bess suggested.

"Maybe. But I'm not crossing him off my list just yet." Nancy went on to explain her suspicions about Julian St. James. "I want to check and see if this guy Carl Drew really exists," she ended up. "Maybe I can get Aunt Eloise on it."

George stood up. "You finish your soda, Nan. I'm done with mine—I'll call your aunt." She headed for a phone booth in the corner of the room.

Bess and Nancy were still discussing the Julian St. James connection when George returned and slid into her seat. "Your aunt's going to start looking for Carl Drew," she said. "Meanwhile, she said you got a call from Page Durrell, Nan. She'll see you at six at the New York Museum of Art."

"Great," Nancy said eagerly. "It's five-thirty now—we'd better get going." Nancy wondered why Page Durrell had changed her mind about talking to her. Whatever the reason, she was glad. "Any other news?"

"Your aunt said that she hasn't managed to find Aristotle Kiriakis yet," George said. "Oh, and Officer Jordan called. He reported that your dad hasn't used any of his credit cards since Tuesday at lunch. Plus, he took a look around your dad's hotel suite this morning, and he didn't notice anything suspicious."

Nancy fell silent as she considered this information. Neither she nor the police seemed to be any
closer to finding her father, she thought. He
father had disappeared Tuesday afternoon. It wa
now Friday evening. The more time passed, th
more Nancy feared that something terrible migh
have happened to him.

"Hey, Nan—didn't Judge Tremain say something about putting pressure on the police to fin
your dad?" Bess spoke up. "I wonder if he calle
Officer Jordan. . . ." When Nancy didn't reply
Bess touched her arm. "Nan? What's the matter?

Nancy turned to Bess, her blue eyes troubled. '
just had this horrible idea—what if Dad's bee
kidnapped?"

Bess frowned. "If that were so, wouldn't w
have gotten a ransom note by now? It's been thre
days."

"That's right," George added reassuringly. "I'n
sure your dad's okay."

"I suppose so," Nancy said slowly. But inside
she was far from sure.

"So you see, I'm afraid I can't be of much hel
to you," Page Durrell told Nancy and her friend

Nancy, Bess, and George were sitting in M
Durrell's office on the top floor of the New Yo
Museum of Art. In her early forties, the curate
had light blond hair, which she wore knotted
the back of her neck. Her old-fashioned-lookin
dress was the same pale blue as her eyes, and he

only accessories were a cameo brooch and a thin gold wristwatch. Nancy noted that she seemed very nervous.

The girls had been talking to her for the last twenty minutes. Her story had been much like Judge Tremain's, Gabriella Ciardi's, and Julian St. James's: Carson Drew had called on Monday asking for an appointment, and she'd given him one for Wednesday at 9 A.M. She'd gotten the impression that he was representing the estate of an art patron who wanted to leave some paintings to the museum. But Wednesday morning had come and gone, and Mr. Drew never showed up. Nor had he called to cancel.

When Ms. Durrell had finished her account, Nancy showed her the list of five names. "Do you know any of these other people?"

The curator took the list from Nancy and studied it. Nancy noticed that her hand was trembling slightly. She definitely seemed nervous—but why?

After a moment Ms. Durrell handed the list back to Nancy. "I don't know any of them, no."

"But what about Gabriella Ciardi? Didn't her magazine interview you once?" Bess spoke up.

Ms. Durrell's eyes widened; Nancy thought she detected a touch of fear in them. "Oh, yes," the curator said quickly. "They did interview me, and I did meet Ms. Ciardi—briefly. My mistake."

"What about the falcon?" George asked her, pointing to the sketch. "Does that ring a bell?"

"It, um, might be a gargoyle or a crest of some sort," Ms. Durrell said, barely glancing at the sketch. "Really, I don't know."

Nancy silently regarded the curator. It wasn't her imagination—Ms. Durrell was more than a little uneasy. Did she know something about Nancy's dad?

Nancy stood up. She knew she wouldn't get any more answers out of Ms. Durrell. "Well, thank you for your time," she said. "If you remember anything else, you have my number."

Ms. Durrell stood up, too, and reached for a cane. "A sprained ankle," she explained hastily. "Let me walk you out to the hall so I can show you the best way out. It's after hours at this point, and the museum will be quite dark."

After saying goodbye to Ms. Durrell, Nancy and her friends followed the route she'd indicated. The museum was huge, and in the semidarkness it looked eerie. As they passed through the Old Masters room, dozens of portraits seemed to stare down at them.

"This is spooky," Bess said, shivering. "Those paintings are watching us."

"I think it's kind of fun," George said with a grin. "I can't believe Ms. Durrell is letting us walk through the museum without a guard, though. I mean, what if we were art thieves or something?"

"This museum has a really high-tech security system," Nancy told her. "I've been here before.

If we touched one of those paintings, all kinds of alarms would go off."

After they passed through the Old Masters room, they reached the Arms and Armor room. Swords, axes, and shields were hung on the stone walls, and suits of armor stood like statues.

Bess began speeding up. "This is even spookier than the other room," she moaned. "Come on, guys, let's get out of here."

"You are such a chicken," George chided her.

"I see what Bess means," Nancy said, glancing around. "Look at those suits of armor. People used to die in them. And this other stuff—"

Just then Nancy heard a creaking noise to her left. She whirled around but not in time. She screamed in horror. A heavy suit of armor was crashing down toward her!

7

Kidnapped!

"Nancy!" Bess shrieked.

Nancy knew instinctively that it was too late to get out of the way. She threw her arms up, trying to protect her head and face. But the heavy metal-plated armor hit her shoulder with its full weight, knocking her down. She lay pinned to the floor beneath it, groaning with pain.

George was on her knees in an instant, trying to heave the armor off her friend. "Bess, help me! Nancy, are you hurt?" she added worriedly.

"I-I'm not sure," Nancy mumbled weakly. As George and Bess worked to free her, Nancy thought she heard muffled footsteps receding into the distance. She tried to figure out where they were coming from. The suit of armor had been positioned next to an open doorway; just beyond the doorway was a dark corridor.

60

"Do you guys hear that?" Nancy whispered.

George and Bess stopped what they were doing. "You mean those footsteps?" George whispered back after a moment.

"That's right. What if someone was hiding in the corridor and pushed the suit of armor onto me?" Nancy mused. "Come on, girls, hurry and get this thing off me. We've got to go after that person!"

When Nancy was free, George gave her a hand and helped her up. "Are you okay? Do you think anything's broken?"

"We'd better get you to a doctor right away," Bess added anxiously.

Nancy swiftly felt for broken bones. There didn't seem to be any, though she could tell that she'd have some nasty bruises later on. "There's no time for a doctor," she said. "Come on!"

"I don't know——" Bess protested, but Nancy was already loping down the dark corridor.

As Nancy ran, she noticed that the floor wasn't carpeted. Why hadn't she heard the person sneak up behind the suit of armor? The only explanation was that the person had been there all along, waiting to ambush the girls as they walked through the Arms and Armor room. But who could it have been? Not Page Durrell—she had a sprained ankle, and there was no way she could have beaten the girls to that spot, though she *had* been awfully nervous during their meeting.

Then another thought occurred to Nancy:

Where were the guards? Why hadn't one of them heard the commotion and come rushing to the scene? And what about the alarm system?

Nancy stopped for a second as they came to an intersection of two corridors. Off to the right was something called the Pritchard Hall of Medieval Art. Off to the left was the sculpture wing. Nancy thought she could hear a faint sound coming from that direction. "This way," she told the girls, pointing to the left.

They entered the sculpture wing, which was an enormous hall with high ceilings. A few dim lights were on, casting an eerie glow over the marble and bronze figures ranged around the room.

Bess stopped suddenly and screamed. Nancy whirled around. "What is it?" she cried out.

"It's him! Oh, no, it's not him." Bess had almost run into a tall bronze statue of a man. "I guess I'm kind of jumpy," she said apologetically.

The girls continued through the gallery. The dim lights threw strange shadows on the stone walls; looking at them, Nancy felt a shiver go up her spine.

Snap out of it, Drew, she chided herself. They're only statues.

Just then Nancy heard something that made her stop short. There were footsteps coming toward them from the next room. It seemed as though her attacker was doubling back!

Nancy grabbed George and Bess and steered

them toward a massive sculpture. "Quick, hide!" she whispered fiercely.

"What do you three think you're doing?"

Nancy glanced in the direction of the husky voice. She saw a shadowy figure walking through the room toward them. In an instant she realized that it was a guard.

Good, she thought with relief. Finally, we'll get some backup.

Nancy ran over to the guard and quickly told him what had happened. When she'd finished, he frowned at her suspiciously. "You say you had an appointment with Ms. Durrell?" he said. "I'm going to have to check on that."

"But there's no time!" Nancy said urgently. "That person's going to get away!"

"*If* this person even exists." The guard walked over to a phone on the wall, dialed a number, and spoke into it. A moment later he hung up and said, "Ms. Durrell's not in her office. She's probably gone home for the day. But the guard out front says you're down on his list as having an appointment with her, so I guess that part of your story checks out."

"Will you help us find Nancy's attacker?" George asked him.

"I'm going to help you leave the museum," the guard replied curtly. "If there's anyone in this building who's not authorized to be here, we'll take care of it ourselves." He nodded toward an

Exit sign. "Follow me. And on the way I'll have to take your names, addresses, and phone numbers, just in case it turns out you're all lying to me."

"But we're *not* lying to you," Nancy said angrily. "I was attacked in this museum, and it's your job to do something about it!"

"I *am* going to do something about it," the guard told her. "I'll see that this matter is investigated. But for right now, you'll have to leave."

The guard escorted the girls to the front entrance of the museum. Nancy tried to argue him into letting them stay, but to no avail. After giving him their names, addresses, and phone numbers, Nancy and her friends walked out into the street.

Outside, it had started to rain softly. The sky was a dark blue-gray, and the air was heavy and cold. Pulling her jean jacket more tightly around herself, Nancy said, "Well, *that* was frustrating. Not only did we lose the person who did that to us, but the guard didn't seem to believe our story!"

"What I want to know is, who could it have been?" George murmured. "Do you think one of our suspects tailed us here, Nan?"

Nancy looked thoughtful. Out of Miguel Lopez, Cassie Dake, Quito Messenger, Julian St. James, the gray-haired man from Chinatown, and the woman with the red sunglasses, who could have known Nancy and her friends would be at the museum?

"Maybe the person really wants you off the

case," Bess spoke up, looking worried. "Maybe he or she doesn't want you to find your dad."

"Well, there's no way I'm going to stop looking," Nancy replied firmly. "Besides—" She paused and pointed to a cab that was parked about fifty feet away. A gray-haired man was getting into the backseat. For one brief second he glanced over his shoulder in the girls' direction.

"That's the guy who was following us around Chinatown!" Nancy cried out. She started running toward the cab.

But just as she reached it, the cab pulled away, its tires screeching loudly. Nancy put her hands on her hips and stared after it in frustration.

Bess and George came running up beside her. "Do you think he was the one who pushed the suit of armor?" Bess asked her breathlessly.

"Maybe," Nancy replied, gazing at the cab as it disappeared down the street. "I'm positive now that he's involved in the business with Dad." She added, "But who is he? And what does he want with us?"

"I've got good news and bad news," Aunt Eloise announced. She, Nancy, George, and Bess were having dinner in Marie's Kitchen, an Italian restaurant near her apartment. It was a small, cozy place with red-and-white-checkered tableclothes, candles, and tiny Christmas lights adorning the frescoed walls.

"First the bad news," Nancy's aunt went on. "I

65

can't find Carl Drew anywhere. I tried phone books, old newspapers—I even tried calling a couple of the theater guilds to see if they had information on him. And I came up totally empty-handed."

Nancy took a bite of her fettuccine carbonara. "I'm starting to think Julian St. James just made him up for some reason," she said. "I'll bet that handkerchief we found *was* Dad's. I wish I hadn't given it back to Mr. St. James." Nancy turned to her aunt. "So what's the good news?"

"The good news is, I found Aristotle Kiriakis," Aunt Eloise replied. "I called a bunch of Kiriakises in the phone book, pretending to be looking for my old college classmate Aristotle. I managed to find some uncle of his, who told me that Aristotle is the chief administrator of Manhattan General Hospital. He's also a doctor, but he doesn't practice, although he does some research."

Nancy patted her aunt on the shoulder. "That's terrific detective work, Aunt Eloise!" she said excitedly.

Aunt Eloise beamed. "I was rather proud of it myself."

"We can call Manhattan General first thing tomorrow," Nancy said. "If we're lucky, he'll be working there, even though it's Saturday. Speaking of calls, did someone named Cassie Dake call sometime this afternoon?"

Her aunt frowned. "No—why?"

"There might be a connection between her and a lawyer Dad met with earlier this week," Nancy explained. "I hope she calls soon. Otherwise, I'll have to try to track her down, too."

Bess twirled some spinach linguine around her fork. "Don't forget—the *Bellissima* party is tomorrow night. We'll be sure to see her there."

"That's true," Nancy agreed.

After dessert the foursome headed back to Aunt Eloise's apartment. Nancy was anxious to get home, in case the police called with news about her father.

When they got there, the phone was ringing. "I'll get that!" Nancy called out as they walked through the door. She rushed over to the phone and picked it up. "Hello?"

"Is this the Drew residence?"

The voice was muffled and low. A prickle of apprehension ran down Nancy's spine. "Yes— who is this?"

"Never mind who this is," the voice went on menacingly. "I've got Carson Drew. And if you ever want to see him alive again, it's going to cost you a quarter of a million dollars."

8

The Incident in the Morgue

Nancy gasped. She couldn't believe what she was hearing. "A . . . quarter of a million dollars?" she repeated. Out of the corner of her eye, she could see Aunt Eloise, George, and Bess watching her intently.

"You'll receive further instructions soon," the gruff voice went on. "In the meantime, don't tell anyone about any of this, especially the cops—or you can kiss your Mr. Drew goodbye permanently."

"Wait!" Nancy fought aside her panic. The more she talked to this person, the better chance she had of picking up clues. "Is he okay?" she asked. "I'd like some proof that you really have him—and that he's alive." Her voice shook on that last word.

"I'll send you proof in a day or so," the man said

with an ominous chuckle. "I'll be in touch." Then he hung up.

Nancy put the phone down slowly, then turned to her aunt. "That—that was some man who says he's got Dad," she said. It took an enormous effort to keep her voice steady. "He wants a quarter of a million dollars in ransom money."

"What!" Aunt Eloise cried out. "Carson's been kidnapped?" She looked as though she were about to faint.

George took her arm and helped her onto the couch, while Bess disappeared into the kitchen to fetch her a glass of water.

"I don't understand," Aunt Eloise said, sounding agitated. "Why would anyone want to kidnap Carson? I know, he makes a good living, but he doesn't have a quarter of a million dollars lying around."

"I know—it's weird." Nancy sat down beside her aunt and tried to focus her thoughts.

Bess returned with a glass of water. Aunt Eloise took a sip, then sat up straight. "We have to call the police right away," she said, looking determined.

"I'm not sure that's a good idea," Nancy said quickly. She repeated what the kidnapper had said about contacting the police. "I don't want to endanger Dad's life in any way."

"But what are you going to do, Nan?" Bess asked worriedly. "I mean, there's no way you can come up with a quarter of a million dollars, right? The only solution is to find your dad—fast."

Nancy was silent as she considered this. If this had happened to a client of hers, she would probably advise him or her to take the risk of calling the police. But with her own father's life at stake, she felt much less nervy.

"I want to wait until we get proof this guy really does have Dad," she said finally. "If we haven't found Dad by Sunday, then we'll call the police."

"I'm not sure I like this," Aunt Eloise began doubtfully.

Just then the phone rang again. Nancy jumped up to get it. "It could be the kidnapper," she said apprehensively. She picked up the phone. "Hello?"

"Nancy?" It was a woman's voice. "This is Cassie Dake. I got your message to call."

Nancy took a deep breath, then glanced at the others and shook her head. "Hi, Cassie," she went on. "Thanks for calling me back."

"Sorry I couldn't do it sooner, but the dragon lady had me running around in circles all day," Cassie said with a giggle. "I'm still at the office, in fact. I'm on my way out to meet some friends at a cool new club, though. You guys want to come?"

"No, thanks," Nancy said. "We're kind of tied up here with something." She added, "The reason I asked you to call is, I was wondering how you knew Miguel Lopez."

70

There was a brief silence. "Miguel Lopez? Who's Miguel Lopez? Oh, yeah, he's that new singer with the Roach Babies, right?"

"Um, no," Nancy said. "You see, when I was at your office, I noticed you had a message on your desk to call him. I think he's an old friend of our family's, and I'm trying to track him down," she fibbed.

"You must have made a mistake," Cassie told her. "There wasn't any message for me from Miguel Lopez. I don't even know anyone by that name—except the Roach Babies guy, and of course I don't know him in person, although I wish I did. He's so cute."

Nancy frowned. Why would Cassie lie about knowing Mr. Lopez? Nancy had seen his name and phone number written on the message slip, clear as day.

Cassie's voice cut into her thoughts. "Listen, I've got to run. You're coming to the party tomorrow night, right?"

"Right," Nancy replied.

"I'll see you there, then. 'Bye," Cassie said. "And good luck finding this Lopez person."

After hanging up, Nancy relayed the call to her aunt and her friends. "Maybe you did make a mistake," Bess said when she'd finished. "Maybe it wasn't Miguel Lopez's name on the message."

"I'm positive it was," Nancy told her firmly. "The question is, why is Cassie covering it up?"

* * *

71

Later that night Nancy tossed and turned in bed for hours. She couldn't stop thinking about her father and wondering if he was okay. And wondering if she'd be able to find him before his kidnappers hurt him—or worse.

Now that she knew kidnapping was in the picture, she was sure there was more than one culprit. She went over her suspect list. The gray-haired man was definitely involved; he'd followed the girls on Friday afternoon, and he'd been at the museum after the suit of armor incident. But who was he? Who was he working with? And why was he tailing her and her friends?

There was also the woman with the red sunglasses who'd been outside her father's hotel suite Thursday night. Maybe Mr. Lambert was right, though, and she was a guest who'd simply found herself on the wrong floor. So what about Julian St. James—was he lying about Carl Drew and the business of the handkerchief? And why had Quito Messenger become so unfriendly so quickly? And of course, there was Miguel Lopez and Cassie Dake . . .

And what was the significance of the falcon drawing she'd found in her father's suite?

When Nancy finally fell asleep at three o'clock, she still had no answers.

Saturday morning was rainy and gloomy. As Nancy finished her breakfast, she stared out the window at the overcast gray sky and the raindrops pelting against the pane. Thoughts of her father weighed heavily on her mind.

George sat down next to her, a glass of orange juice in hand. She'd just returned from a three-mile run. "You look tired, Nan," George said sympathetically. "No sleep?"

"Not much," Nancy replied, smiling wanly. "But I'll manage. There's a lot to do today. First, I want to call Manhattan General and track down Aristotle Kiriakis. I also want to zero in on Carl Drew. Plus, we have to head over to the Imperial Hotel and pick up Dad's stuff. Today is his official check-out day." Tears began to well in her eyes, but she brushed them away.

Nancy got up briskly and headed for the phone. "It's eight-thirty; maybe I'll try the hospital now."

After being transferred several times, Nancy finally got through to a secretary, who told her, "Dr. Kiriakis is in an emergency meeting. Can I take a message?"

"Yes, please ask him to call me." Nancy gave the secretary her name and number. "It's regarding—"

But the woman hung up before Nancy was able to finish her sentence. "Great," she muttered. "Now Aristotle Kiriakis will have no idea why I want to talk to him. It'll probably take him days to call me back—if he ever calls me back at all."

"Maybe we should just head up there and try to see him," George suggested.

Nancy nodded. "That's not a bad idea—unless he's in the meeting all day, of course."

Just then Aunt Eloise and Bess came home from a quick trip to buy fresh hot bagels. As the four of them were chatting over bagels and coffee, the phone rang. Nancy ran to answer it. "Hello?"

"Hi, there—Nancy Drew, please."

Nancy's heart began to race at the unfamiliar man's voice. It didn't sound like the kidnapper from last night—but maybe it was an accomplice?

"This is she," she said.

"Oh, terrific," the man said. "This is Dr. Kiriakis from Manhattan General. I was told that you wanted to speak to me."

"Oh, right." Nancy let out a deep breath. "Thank you for calling me back." She was surprised that he'd returned her call so quickly. But in any case, she was glad.

"I wondered if I could come and see you for a few minutes regarding my father, Carson Drew," Nancy said. "I believe he made an appointment to meet with you earlier this week. He's missing, and I'm very anxious to talk to anyone who may have seen him recently." She didn't explain *how* he happened to be missing, in keeping with the kidnapper's instructions.

"Carson Drew—hmm. The name sounds familiar, but I'm not positive." After a pause Dr. Kiriakis said, "I'll take a peek at my calendar, which unfortunately is in my office in another part of the hospital. But in the meantime, why don't you come by at ten-thirty? Check in with the receptionist at the main entrance—she'll direct you to me."

Nancy let out a sigh of relief. The doctor was being a lot more cooperative than Gabriella Ciardi, Julian St. James, or Page Durrell had been. "Great," she said. "I'll see you at ten-thirty."

Manhattan General was located across the street from Central Park, in a complex of tall, brick buildings. Inside, the lobby was full of activity.

"I hate hospitals," Bess murmured, glancing around. "They're so depressing." Then her face lit up. "Except for all the hunky young interns, of course. Check out that one by the elevator!" She pointed to a blond guy in a green scrub suit.

Nancy walked up to the receptionist. "We're looking for Dr. Aristotle Kiriakis," she explained. "We have an appointment with him at ten-thirty."

The receptionist nodded and rooted through some papers. "Yes—here it is. He left a message for you to meet him in Room fifty-five, which is in Basement Level B. He's doing some work down there."

"Thank you," Nancy said.

The girls took the elevator down to Basement Level B. When they got off, they found themselves in a deserted lime green hallway. The air was cold and mildewy. On either side of the hallway were refrigerators covered with ominous-looking red stickers that said Warning: Biohazard.

"It's creepy down here," Bess remarked.

"What do those red stickers mean?" George asked.

"There are probably dangerous virus samples in there," Nancy replied.

"Dangerous viruses—great." Bess glanced around apprehensively. "Where is everybody, anyway?"

"Who knows?" Nancy studied the numbers on the doors, then pointed to the left. "I think fifty-five is that way—come on."

When they got to the door marked 55, Nancy knocked but got no answer. "I guess we should just wait for him inside," she told her friends.

Nancy turned the knob and walked in. Then she stopped and frowned in confusion. Room 55 didn't look like an office or a hospital room. It was brightly, almost blindingly lit with rows of fluorescent lights. In the center sat a stainless-steel table, with sharp surgical knives lying on top of it. There were drops of blood on the floor, and the air smelled unpleasantly medicinal.

"Is—is this like an operating room or something?" Bess said in a quivering voice. "I don't think I like being in here."

"For once, I agree with you," George said nervously. "I don't like it in here, either."

Then Nancy noticed something else. Off in the corner was another table. And on top of it was a sleeping man.

Curious, Nancy walked over to him—and

gasped. The man's skin was bluish white, and his eyes were bulging and lifeless. He wasn't sleeping—he was dead.

Nancy backed away from the table. "Hey, um, guys?" she said slowly. "I—I don't think we're in an operating room. I—I think we're in the morgue."

Bess clamped her hand on her mouth to stifle a scream, then ran to the door. "I'm not staying in here another second—" she began. But when she tried to open the door, it wouldn't budge.

She whirled around, her blue eyes wide with alarm. "Nancy! George! The door's locked!" she cried out. "We're trapped in here!"

9

A Wild Chase

"What!" Nancy exclaimed.

Bess began banging frantically on the morgue door. "Help!" she shouted. "Somebody get us out of here!"

"I—I can't believe we're stuck in here with a dead body," George said shakily. She glanced at the corpse lying on the table, then looked around the room. "And there's no phone in here, so we can't call anyone to get us out."

Nancy took a deep breath to calm herself, then walked up to Bess. "Here, let me try that door. Maybe it's just stuck or something."

Bess moved aside instantly. "Be my guest. Just get us out of here."

Nancy put her hand on the knob to jiggle it. The door was definitely stuck. "Maybe I can try using

78

the tools in my lockpicking kit," she said, reaching into her purse.

But after half an hour of working with her tools, Nancy was unable to pry the door open. "I give up," she announced to her friends, who were hovering nearby, shivering in the chilly air. "I guess we'll just have to wait for someone to get us out of here."

"No one's come down here yet," George pointed out worriedly. "What if we're trapped in here all day—and all night?"

"I don't know—" Nancy began, then fell silent. Were those footsteps she heard out in the hallway.

She began banging on the door. "Help! Help, get us out of here!" she yelled.

A moment later the knob began to rattle from the other side. The door opened.

Nancy found herself staring at a middle-aged man dressed in jeans, a black football jersey, and a white lab coat. He was big and bearlike, with curly brown hair and a bushy beard.

He stared at her in amazement. "Who are you? And what are you doing in here?"

"I'm Nancy Drew, and I have an appointment with Dr. Aristotle Kiriakis," Nancy explained. "The receptionist told us we could find him in here. But then the door got stuck—"

"I'm Dr. Kiriakis," the man cut in. He sighed and shook his head. "I told the receptionist Room Fifty-six. She must have written it down wrong."

Bess scurried past them and went out the door. "I don't know about the rest of you," she said, "but I'd rather be having this meeting somewhere else."

Dr. Kiriakis frowned at her. "Who's she?"

"That's Bess Marvin. And this"—Nancy nodded toward George—"is George Fayne. I asked them to come with me. I hope that's okay."

"No problem. The more the merrier—although that's kind of a weird thing to say in a morgue, isn't it?" The doctor chuckled at his own gruesome joke, then pointed to Room 56, across the hallway. "Come this way. I'm sorry about this door—it gets stuck sometimes. The trick is, you have to lift up the knob before you turn it."

"Shouldn't you get it fixed?" George suggested.

Dr. Kiriakis laughed. "I'll make a note of it."

He opened the door to Room 56. It appeared to be a laboratory; the long black counters were covered with glass beakers, and off in the corner was a large sink. "I asked you to meet me down here rather than in my office because I had some lab work to look over," he explained. "I hope you don't mind. Please, grab a stool."

Nancy and her friends did so. Then Nancy pulled the list of five names out of her purse and held it out to the doctor. "My father disappeared four days ago," she began. "We found this in his hotel suite, and that's why I contacted you."

Dr. Kiriakis studied the list. "I see," he said

80

after a moment. "I checked my calendar after you called, by the way. Your dad *did* call me to ask for an appointment—on Monday, or maybe Tuesday. I told him to come and see me on Wednesday at three. But he never made it."

Nancy, Bess, and George exchanged troubled glances. That's five out of five, Nancy thought. Five names on the list . . . five appointments made and not kept . . .

"Did he call you to cancel?" Nancy asked, already knowing the answer.

"No." Dr. Kiriakis stroked his beard thoughtfully. "What's his interest in hospital administration?"

Nancy started. "None that I know of."

The doctor shrugged. "I just assumed that's why he made an appointment. Why else would he want to see me?"

"How about the other people on this list?" George spoke up. "Do you know them?"

Dr. Kiriakis studied the list a second time. "This Tremain guy is running for mayor or governor or something, right?" he said. "As for the others—no."

"How about the falcon?" Bess added. "Does it mean anything to you?"

Dr. Kiriakis nodded. "Of course."

"It does?" Nancy said eagerly. Finally someone knew something about the bird sketch!

The doctor beamed. "The Atlanta Falcons are

81

my favorite football team. I guess they must be your dad's, too."

"I still can't believe we were locked in a morgue," Bess said gloomily.

She, Nancy, and George were sitting on a bench in Central Park. They'd decided to buy a quick lunch of hot dogs and sodas from a pushcart before heading off to the Imperial Hotel to pick up Mr. Drew's belongings.

It had stopped raining, and the sky was a pale, pearly gray. Spring was in full bloom in the park. Bright yellow daffodils bloomed everywhere, as well as red and orange tulips and bushes of golden forsythia. Since it was Saturday, the park was crowded with people: joggers, walkers, in-line skaters, and parents pushing baby strollers.

George took a bite of her hot dog, then turned to Nancy. "So what did you think of Dr. Kiriakis?"

"He seemed like a nice enough guy," Nancy said. "The question is, why did Dad want to see him? And why did he stand him up without canceling, just as he did with the others on the list?" She shook her head in frustration. "I wish there was a connection between the five people to explain all this, but I don't see one. I mean, they're in totally different professions: a judge, a magazine editor, a Broadway director, a museum curator, and a surgeon. Of course, it's possible the list has nothing to do with Dad's kidnapping."

"Maybe not," George said. "But the whole thing is so weird!"

"Hey, guys? Speaking of weird . . ." Bess nodded nervously at a nearby grove of trees. "Isn't that our gray-haired friend over there? You know, the one who's been following us around?"

Nancy looked quickly in the direction Bess indicated. She was right—the gray-haired man was hiding behind one of the trees. As soon as he realized that he'd been spotted, he turned and began walking rapidly in the opposite direction.

Nancy jumped up and ran after him. "Come on, guys! This time we're going to get some answers!"

The man glanced over his shoulder, then broke into a sprint. He was a surprisingly fast runner. With so many other people on the path, Nancy and her friends had a hard time keeping up with him.

The path went alongside a pond. Coming around a curve, Nancy nearly knocked down a little girl who was sailing a remote-operated toy boat. "I'm so sorry," she apologized, stopping to help the girl regain her balance. The girl's father glared suspiciously at Nancy.

When Nancy glanced around again, the gray-haired man had vanished. "Which way did he go?" she asked her friends. The path ahead of them forked to the right and the left.

"Right!" Bess yelled.

"Left!" George yelled at the same time.

Nancy frowned. "Come on, guys—which way?"

"We'd better go with George," Bess said sheepishly. "I was kind of busy looking at those cute ducks."

"Bess!" George exclaimed in annoyance.

The three of them continued running. After a few hundred feet the path entered a long tunnel. Nancy slowed down as she entered it. It was dark and cavernous, with graffiti spray-painted on the damp, moldy walls. There was no one else inside it.

Then Nancy heard the echo of footsteps just ahead. "Hello?" she called out.

"This is spooky," Bess whispered behind her. "What if it's a mugger or something? Let's get out of here!"

"Hello?" Nancy called out again. The sound of the footsteps had stopped, and as far as she could tell, there was no one in the tunnel up ahead. "That's strange," she muttered to herself. "Come on, let's keep moving," she added to her friends.

They emerged from the tunnel and continued down the path. After a few minutes they came to a large lawn full of sunbathers and picnickers. Nancy stopped and looked around. "Do you guys see him?"

"In this crowd? No way." George sighed. "He might not even have stayed on this path. He could have taken a detour."

"I think we've lost him for good," Nancy murmured in frustration. "I guess we'd better give up and head over to the Imperial Hotel." She shook her head. "I still don't get it, though. If the gray-haired man is one of Dad's kidnappers, why is he following us? It doesn't make sense."

Bess frowned. "I just had an awful idea, Nan. What if he wants to kidnap you, too?"

Nancy felt a shiver go up her spine. What if Bess was right?

"So what's on the agenda for the rest of the day?" George said.

The girls were in the elevator of the Imperial Hotel, riding up to Mr. Drew's suite. It was one o'clock, an hour past the official checkout time, but Mr. Lambert had told them that it was no problem.

"After we drop Dad's stuff off at Aunt Eloise's, I'd like to head over to the Gotham Theater," Nancy replied. "I have an idea how we can find out more about Carl Drew. And after that, we've got some free time before the *Bellissima* party." She added, "I'm glad Cassie will be there. I really want to find out why she lied to me about not knowing Miguel Lopez."

The girls headed down the hall to Suite 312. Nancy took the key out of her pocket and unlocked the door.

"This is so depressing," Nancy said, her voice

quavering slightly. "Having to pack up Dad's stuff, I mean. I thought—I thought we would have found him by now."

Bess put her arm around Nancy's shoulders. "I know. But we'll find him soon—I'm sure of it."

Nancy nodded, then pushed open the door and went into the suite.

She wasn't prepared for the sight that greeted her.

The living room was a total mess. Furniture had been turned upside-down, and her father's clothes and other belongings were scattered all over the floor. The couch had been slit open with a knife— it was covered with savage-looking slash marks.

"Someone's broken in!" Nancy cried out.

10

Armed and Dangerous

Who could have done this to her dad's hotel room? Nancy wondered in horror. Was it one of his kidnappers?

Bess touched Nancy's elbow. "I think we should get out of here," she whispered nervously. "I mean, what if the burglar's still in there?"

"Good point," Nancy whispered back. "You guys stay here—I'm going to take a look around and make sure we're alone."

"But, Nan—" George protested.

Nancy put a finger to her lips. Then, moving as quietly as possible, she checked out the living room, then the bedroom, then the bathroom.

There was no one hiding in the closets or under the bed or behind the shower curtain. In each room, however, the intruder had left his or her mark. Everything was in a shambles; even the mattress had been slashed open.

"Coast is clear!" Nancy called out from the bedroom. "Don't touch anything, okay? There may be fingerprints."

Bess and George joined her. "Who do you think did this?" George said, glancing around in dismay.

"I suppose it must have been Dad's kidnappers," Nancy said slowly. "But why would they do such a thing? They already have Dad." She added, "Let's get Mr. Lambert up here, then call the police."

"But that man who called last night said we weren't supposed to get the police involved," Bess reminded her quickly.

"I know," Nancy said. "But Mr. Lambert will insist on it. The question is, should we mention the kidnapper's call to the police?"

"That's totally up to you, Nan," George told her gently. "It's your father we're talking about."

Nancy nodded, then began pacing around the room. She didn't want to endanger her father's life, and the kidnapper had explicitly warned her not to talk to the police . . . or else. But she was beginning to feel that she couldn't hold out on the authorities any longer.

Just then she spotted something out of the corner of her eye. Under one of the overturned chairs lay a pair of red, cat's-eye-shaped sunglasses.

Nancy pulled a tissue out of her purse, wrapped her hand in it, then picked up the sunglasses carefully, so as not to smear any fingerprints. "Look familiar?" she asked George.

"Those are the sunglasses that woman was wearing," George said at once.

"Woman? What woman?" Bess asked, confused.

"The woman we saw outside the door here on Thursday night," Nancy explained. She turned the sunglasses over and glanced at the name of the maker. "Whoever it is, she has expensive tastes," she added, noting the famous designer brand.

"Do you think she's working together with the gray-haired man?" George said thoughtfully.

"It's beginning to look like it," Nancy said. "I still don't get it, though. Why are they doing all this stuff—following us and breaking into Dad's suite, I mean—*after* they've already kidnapped him?"

"I don't know, and I don't like it," Bess replied with a frown.

Nancy put the sunglasses in her purse. Then, keeping the tissue wrapped around her hand, she picked up the phone and made two calls: one to Mr. Lambert and one to the police.

Mr. Lambert came up immediately. He was upset to see the state of the room. "I—I don't understand," he murmured. "How could such a thing happen in my hotel?"

"Do you know when the maids were in here last?" Nancy asked him. "That would help pinpoint the time of the break-in."

"The maids haven't been in here since Tuesday

morning," Mr. Lambert replied. "I told them to leave the suite alone, since Mr. Drew hadn't returned."

Nancy nodded. "So the last one in here was Officer Jordan, yesterday morning," she said. "That means that the break-in could have happened anytime between then and now."

Several minutes later a husky police officer with salt-and-pepper hair arrived. He introduced himself as Officer Jordan.

"I've been handling your father's case," he told Nancy. He glanced around the suite and clicked his tongue. "Looks like someone took a machete to this place. It wasn't like this when I was here yesterday." He added, "By the way, I just checked the lock. There's no sign that it was picked. That means the perpetrator must have had a key."

Nancy was silent as she considered this. If indeed her father had been kidnapped, one of the kidnappers could have entered the suite using her father's key.

Then Nancy remembered something. "Did Judge Tremain ever call you?" she asked Officer Jordan. "He was going to talk to the police about this case."

Officer Jordan looked confused. "No—not as far as I know."

Nancy frowned. That's strange, she thought. Judge Tremain promised yesterday that he would call the police.

The policeman's voice cut into Nancy's

thoughts. "I understand that you and Ms. Fayne came by here on Thursday night. Did you notice anything then that's missing now?"

"It's hard to tell," Nancy replied. "The place is such a mess. But Dad didn't have much in here—just some clothes, his suitcase, and some odds and ends."

Officer Jordan nodded, then scribbled something on a pad. After asking a few more questions, he began looking around and dusting for finger-prints.

"There are too many sets of prints in here," he remarked. "You've got Mr. Drew, several previous occupants, half a dozen maids—and probably the two of you." He nodded at Nancy and George.

Nancy and George glanced at each other. "I'm sure we touched some stuff on Thursday," George said.

Officer Jordan packed up his fingerprinting kit. "I'm going to question some of the staff," he said. Then he paused and fixed his eyes on Nancy. "Do you have any idea who might have done this?"

Nancy met his look. "Yes," she said after a moment. "That is, I have a good guess." She told him about the woman she and George had seen outside Mr. Drew's suite on Thursday night. Then she told him about the kidnapper's call.

Officer Jordan stared at her in amazement. "Why didn't you let us know about the kid-napper's call right away?" he said, sounding angry.

"I'm really sorry about that," Nancy apologized. "But the man told me that I'd never see my father alive again if I told anyone about his call, especially the police."

Officer Jordan shook his head, then reached for the phone. "I'm putting in an order to have your aunt's phone tapped," he told Nancy. "After I'm through, I'll have to ask you some more questions."

Nancy sat down on the bed as she waited for Officer Jordan to finish. *Did I do the right thing in telling him about the kidnapper's call?* she asked herself worriedly. *If any harm comes to Dad because of this, I'll never forgive myself.*

It was nearly three o'clock by the time Nancy and her friends got to the Gotham Theater. Nancy had been silent all the way from the Imperial Hotel to the theater. She couldn't stop thinking about her father.

"So what's the plan?" Bess asked Nancy as they stood on the sidewalk outside of the theater.

Nancy was studying the poster next to the box office. It was all black, with white Gothic-looking lettering. It read:

DEADLY SECRETS

A Mystery by James Kunstler
Directed by Julian St. James

Starring Matthew Dimchik, Tony Paglio,
Quito Messenger, and Jennifer Armstrong
Opening April 22

Nancy turned around. "Hmm?"

"What's our plan?" Bess repeated. "You said
something before about getting more info on Carl
Drew." She added, "I don't get it, anyway. If
you're convinced that your dad was kidnapped by
the gray-haired man and the woman with the
sunglasses, why are you bothering with your other
suspects?"

"We can't be sure of anything yet," Nancy
replied. "And what if there are more than two
people involved? I can't ignore the fact that Julian
St. James, Quito, Cassie, and Miguel Lopez have
all been acting suspiciously."

"So how are you going to get dirt on Carl
Drew?" George asked her.

"Very carefully." Nancy glanced around, then
noticed an alley next to the building. "Let's see if
this place has a side entrance, okay?"

"I don't like the sound of this," Bess murmured
nervously.

Down the alley about twenty feet, Nancy found
an unmarked green door. She tried to open it, but
it was locked. She reached into her purse, pulled
out her lockpicking kit, and began working on the
lock surreptitiously.

"Nan!" Bess whispered frantically. "What if
someone sees you?"

"If you guys stand on either side of me, no one will see me," Nancy said confidently.

After a moment she had the lock undone. She pressed her ear up against the door to see if anyone was on the other side. When she couldn't hear anything, she slowly opened the door and went inside.

She found herself in a small, dark area piled high with boxes. Beyond that was a doorway leading to a dimly lit hallway.

"Follow me," Nancy whispered to her friends.

But just as Nancy reached the doorway, she heard a loud crashing noise behind her. She whirled around.

Bess was sprawled out on the floor. "Sorry," she said sheepishly. "I, um, tripped over a box."

George grabbed her cousin's hand and boosted her up. "That's okay," she said cheerfully. "If we get caught, we can blame it on you."

Nancy grinned, then turned and glanced in the hallway. It was deserted. "I think we're safe," she said in a low voice. "Come on, let's go."

Nancy managed to find Julian St. James's office, at the end of the hall. The door was open, but there was no one inside. In the distance she could hear the faint sound of the director's voice, barking out orders. His English accent was unmistakable. "Rehearsal must be going on," she remarked to her friends.

"Um, Nan?" Bess said uneasily. "You're not

thinking of going through his desk and stuff, are you?"

"Just for a second," Nancy reassured her. "You guys be lookouts out here, okay? If anyone comes, distract him. If it's Mr. St. James, act as if we had an appointment with him and we've been waiting for him awhile."

"Got it," George said.

Nancy entered the office and flicked a light on. The room looked much as it had the other day. She spotted what she was looking for at once: Julian St. James's address book, sitting on his desk. Without wasting a second, she went for the "D" section.

"Drabble, Drake, Drenka's Dry Cleaning, Dreyfus . . . no Drew." Nancy frowned. "If Carl Drew is one of this show's backers, why doesn't Mr. St. James have his number?" she said out loud.

She spent a few more minutes looking through the director's desk. There were very few things on it: a legal pad full of rehearsal notes, business letters, a telephone bill marked Overdue, and an alumni magazine from a place called Hilliard College. She didn't find any clues having to do with Carl Drew or her father.

Bess popped her head in. "Are you done yet?" she asked nervously. "I think someone might be coming, but I'm not sure."

"I'm done," Nancy told her. She flicked off the light off and joined her friends in the hallway. "Let's get out of here."

The three of them started in the direction of the exit. But suddenly Nancy realized that they weren't alone. She could hear footsteps coming up behind them.

She whirled around. Quito was marching toward them, and he looked angry.

"Quito—" Nancy began. Then her voice caught in her throat when she saw what Quito was holding in his hand.

It was a gun!

11

Mystery on Board

Bess saw the gun and screamed.

Quito glared at her, then turned his hostile gaze on Nancy. "What are you all doing back here?"

Nancy's mind was racing. How could the three of them get away from Quito without getting hurt?

She decided to stall for time. "We're looking for Mr. St. James," she said after a moment. "We want to talk to him."

Quito narrowed his eyes. "About what?"

"About my father," Nancy replied. Then she pointed to the gun. "What are you going to do with that? If you're planning to shoot us, I don't think that's such a great idea. This place is full of people . . ."

Quito glanced down at his gun. His tough expression disappeared, and he broke into an

97

amused smile. "You thought this was real? No wonder you all were acting so freaked out." He added, "It's a prop gun. I have to kill someone in my next scene."

"Oh." Bess frowned at him. "You don't have to sound so cheerful about it."

Quito stared at her for a moment, then turned his attention back to Nancy. "So you were looking for Julian, huh? He's in rehearsal."

"I figured that out," Nancy said quickly. "Actually, since you're here, there are some questions I'd like to—"

"Sorry, gotta get onstage." Quito stuffed the gun into his jeans pocket and hurried past the girls. "My scene's coming up. See you all later."

"He did it again," Nancy murmured after he'd gone. "Unless I'm wrong, he's definitely avoiding us."

"You think he's hiding something, Nan?" George asked her.

"He sure is acting like it," Nancy said thoughtfully. "The question is, what?"

"I think I've died and gone to heaven," Bess said, sighing happily. "I can't believe we're at a *Bellissima* party!"

She, George, and Nancy—along with Eloise Drew, who'd decided to come along at the last minute—had just boarded the S.S. *Serena*, where the party was in full swing. The *Serena* was docked at a marina on the Hudson River, which ran along the west side of Manhattan.

Inside the lavishly decorated ballroom were hundreds of people, many of them models and other celebrities. On the stage a six-piece band played a sizzling dance tune. Waiters in black tuxedos glided about with trays of champagne and hors d'oeuvres.

Nancy, Bess, and George were all wearing dresses they'd bought that afternoon. Nancy's was a simple black silk tank dress, Bess's was red with spaghetti straps, and George's was made of dark green taffeta. Aunt Eloise was dressed in a gray-blue tunic with matching pants.

Despite being dressed up, Nancy was too preoccupied to enjoy the party. She was worried about her father, and she was anxious to find Cassie and grill her about Miguel Lopez. "I wonder if Cassie's here yet," she said out loud.

Bess plucked some hors d'oeuvres from the tray of a passing waiter. "Mmm—little quiches. I love little quiches."

George elbowed Nancy. "Speak of the devil . . . look who's coming our way," she whispered.

"Nancy! Bess! George!"

Cassie was walking toward them, smiling and waving. She was dressed in a black studded leather jacket and matching miniskirt, and her red hair was standing up in stiff spikes. "Having fun?" she asked brightly. "The boat's about to take off."

"Where's it going?" Bess asked her between bites of quiche.

"Around the island of Manhattan," Cassie replied. "It's like a sunset cruise thing."

Nancy introduced her to her aunt, then said, "By the way, thanks for the passes." She wanted to keep the conversation light and friendly, and not put Cassie on her guard. She had to bring up the subject of Miguel Lopez slowly and carefully.

"Sure thing." Cassie gave her miniskirt a tug. "Oh, yeah. By the way, I figured out who that Lopez person was."

Nancy was startled. "You did?"

"Yeah," Cassie said, giggling. "See, I kind of have a lot of parking tickets that I kind of forgot to pay. Anyway, my friend Althea told me I had to get a lawyer to deal with it, and her boyfriend, Bing, recommended this guy Lopez. I called him earlier this week, and I guess he called me back on Thursday, but I totally forgot about it."

"Oh." Nancy was silent as she took in this information. Was Cassie telling the truth? she wondered. Cassie seemed sincere, but it was possible that she was a good actress, too.

The girls chatted with her for a few more minutes, then Cassie excused herself to say hi to some friends.

"See, I knew she was innocent," Bess said after she'd left. "She's way too nice to be a criminal— and way too spacey, if you ask me."

"Maybe." Nancy touched her aunt's elbow. "Can I put you to work?"

"Absolutely," Aunt Eloise replied. "What do you want me to do?"

"Follow Cassie around," Nancy explained. "Keep your ears open for any mention of Miguel Lopez—or Dad, for that matter."

Aunt Eloise gave her a little salute and started after Cassie. "Anything to help find Carson," she said. "I'll be very discreet—Cassie will never know I'm around."

Nancy turned to George and Bess. "In the meantime, the three of us can—" Then something caught her attention, and she bit back a gasp of surprise. "What's *he* doing here?"

"Who?" George asked her.

"Judge Tremain." Nancy nodded toward the center of the room, where the judge was talking to some people. "This doesn't seem like his kind of party."

Judge Tremain glanced in Nancy's direction and noticed her watching him. He gave her a friendly wave, then started walking toward her.

Nancy waved back. "Come on, let's go talk to him," she said to her friends.

"Well, well, what a pleasant surprise," the judge said cheerfully when they met up.

"We were just saying the same thing," Nancy replied. "Somehow, this doesn't seem like your sort of event."

"It's my wife," the judge explained. "She loves to drag me to these things." He added, "How is the search for your father going? Have they found his kidnappers yet?"

Nancy froze. She'd never said anything to Judge Tremain about her father being kidnapped.

"What makes you think my father's been kidnapped?" she asked him warily.

The judge looked taken aback. Then he smiled and shrugged. "Oh, well. I just assumed the police would consider that as a strong possibility," he said.

"The police haven't reached any definite conclusions at this stage," Nancy told him carefully.

A middle-aged woman came strolling up to Judge Tremain, bringing with her an overpowering cloud of perfume. She had coppery hair cut in a sleek pageboy and was dressed in a floor-length chartreuse dress. At six feet two, she towered over the judge.

"Darling," she said to him in a loud, effusive voice. "This party is absolutely marvelous. Do you know that the van Halls are here? And the Eichelbergers? And that darling man you used to play tennis with, Charlie West?"

"No, I didn't know that, my dear," Judge Tremain said. He turned to the girls. "This is my wife, Liza Tremain. Liza, this is Nancy Drew, George Fayne, and Bess Marvin."

"So pleased to meet you," Mrs. Tremain

gushed. She grabbed Bess's hand. "Is that dress a Pierro original? It's *marvelous.*"

"It's more like a bargain-basement original," Bess replied, blushing. "I just got it today."

"Personally, I love those bargain places," Mrs. Tremain said in a confidential tone. "If you're clever about fashion, you can find the most marvelous things in them. And speaking of fashion, what do you all think of the latest issue of *Bellissima?* Did you happen to notice the yellow snakeskin evening gown in the 'Out and About' section? It was perfectly horrid and yet perfectly marvelous at the same time, I thought. And what about—"

"I'm sure these girls don't want to hear your opinions on the world of fashion, my dear," her husband interrupted gently.

"Nonsense, darling, of course they do. Oh, waiter, more champagne!" Mrs. Tremain grabbed a glass from a passing waiter, then chattered on. "As I was saying, I was *most* impressed by the article on the new line of junk-store jewelry. . . ."

Five minutes later Mrs. Tremain was still going on with her monologue. Judge Tremain, Nancy, and George eventually managed to excuse themselves. The judge went off to talk to someone he knew, and Nancy and George headed out to the deck for some fresh air.

Nancy glanced over her shoulder. "Mrs. Tremain still has Bess," she noted. "Maybe we should go rescue her."

"Bess can fend for herself," George replied with a grin.

They stepped out onto the deck. A few people were leaning against the brass railing, staring out at the Hudson River. The sun had just begun to set, and the sky was streaked with pale gold and pink hues. Behind them, the lights of Manhattan twinkled enchantingly.

"It's beautiful out here," George said with a sigh.

"It sure is," Nancy agreed. "If only we had Dad back safe and sound, everything would be perfect."

"I'm telling you, this is going too far!"

Nancy was jolted by the sound of the familiar female voice. She glanced around, trying to find its source.

Then she saw something that totally shocked her. About thirty feet away, on a secluded part of the deck, was Gabriella Ciardi. The *Bellissima* editor in chief was having a heated argument— with Julian St. James!

12

A Ship Full of Suspects

What were Gabriella Ciardi and Julian St. James doing together? Nancy wondered curiously. Each of them had claimed not to know the other, and yet here they were, having an intense, angry discussion about something.

George leaned toward her. "Is that who I think it is?" she whispered.

"It sure is," Nancy whispered back.

Nancy watched the pair for a moment. Ms. Ciardi was wearing a strapless indigo blue dress with a matching scarf draped dramatically around her shoulders. Mr. St. James was in the outfit he'd worn the day before: a black turtleneck and black pants. They had lowered their voices, and Nancy had a hard time hearing them. "I think a little eavesdropping is in order," she muttered to

George. "Let's go back into the ballroom and try to sneak up on them."

"Fine with me."

But before Nancy and George could make a move toward the ballroom, Gabriella Ciardi caught sight of them. She stared at them in astonishment. Julian St. James, noticing her sudden silence, turned around and also spotted the girls.

Ms. Ciardi came rushing up to them, followed by the director. She looked angry. "What are you doing here?" she demanded, flinging her indigo scarf over her shoulder. "This party is by invitation only—and I don't remember inviting the two of you."

"Cassie Dake was nice enough to give us some passes," Nancy explained lightly. She glanced at Mr. St. James, then added, "I thought you two didn't know each other."

The fashion editor and the director exchanged glances. Nancy wasn't sure, but she thought she detected a hint of fear in their eyes.

"Actually, we just met," Ms. Ciardi said after a moment. "I'm trying to convince him to do an exclusive interview about his new play."

Mr. St. James cleared his throat. "As I said to you earlier, Ms. Ciardi, I'll think about it and give you a ring on Monday," he said. "Now I think I'll be getting back to the party."

"Good idea." Ms. Ciardi flashed Nancy and George a plastic-looking smile. "Enjoy yourselves," she said coldly, then followed the director into the ballroom.

"What was *that* all about?" George said after they'd left.

"I don't know," Nancy replied thoughtfully. "But I think they were lying. They were having a major fight about something, not a friendly discussion about doing an interview for *Bellissima*." She added, "I have an idea. Why don't you follow Mr. St. James around, and I'll follow Ms. Ciardi? Maybe we'll pick up something useful."

"You're on," George said. "With your aunt following Cassie, we'll have all our suspects covered—well, a lot of them, anyway."

The two girls headed into the ballroom. "Mr. St. James is over by the buffet table," George said, rushing off in that direction. "I'd recognize that blond ponytail anywhere. See you later, Nan."

Alone, Nancy glanced around. Bess was still talking to Judge Tremain's wife—or rather, listening to her and nodding mutely—in the center of the room. Cassie was dancing with some cute young guy to a fast rock number. Aunt Eloise was dancing nearby by herself. When she saw Nancy, she gave her a subtle wink.

Gabriella Ciardi was nowhere to be seen. "Oh, great," Nancy muttered. "I've lost her already. Where could she have gone off to?"

Just then a tall, husky guy bumped into her. "Sorry," he mumbled. Then he stepped back and stared at her, his brown eyes wide with surprise.

It was Quito Messenger. He was dressed in a vintage black tuxedo with a red bowtie and matching cummerbund.

Great, Nancy thought eagerly. Another suspect on board! Out loud, she said, "Hi, Quito—I didn't know you'd be here."

"Well, um, I didn't know you'd be here, either." Quito glanced nervously over his shoulder. "Excuse me, but I've got to meet some—"

Nancy laid her hand on his arm. "Am I imagining things, or are you trying to avoid me?" she asked him bluntly.

"Avoid you?" he asked, blinking his eyes wide. "Why would I avoid you? I don't even know you."

"I've been trying to ask you some questions for the last few days," Nancy declared. "Questions about Carl Drew—plus why you were standing outside Mr. St. James's office while we were in there with him yesterday."

Quito looked edgy. "I don't know what you're talking about," he insisted. "And I don't know this Carl Drew dude. As I said—"

Suddenly a security guard appeared out of nowhere and tapped Quito on the shoulder. "Can I see your invitation, please?"

"Invitation?" Quito repeated, frowning. Then he began searching through his pockets. "I, um, must have left it somewhere," he said after a moment.

"Then I'll have to ask you to come with me, please," the security guard said.

"Why?" Quito demanded.

"Just come with me, please," the guard repeated, more firmly this time.

Quito sighed. "Okay, whatever. But I'm telling you, this is harassment."

Watching Quito follow the guard across the ballroom, Nancy wondered if he had crashed the party.

Everyone was behaving very strangely, she mused: Quito, Cassie, Julian St. James, Gabriella Ciardi. But could she tie their strange behavior to her father's disappearance?

The only person she had any real proof against was Mr. St. James, and even that proof—the blue handkerchief with the initials *CD* on it—wasn't absolute. And all she had against Miguel Lopez, another suspect, was the fact that he and her father were on opposite sides of a case, and that he knew Cassie.

Nancy was sure that the gray-haired man and the woman with the red, cat's-eye sunglasses had been involved in her father's kidnapping. Unfortunately, she had no idea who they were—or how to find them. The only thing she could do was keep pursuing her other suspects. Eventually, she hoped, one or more of them had to provide the key to the mystery.

She caught a flash of indigo out of the corner of her eye: Gabriella Ciardi. The editor in chief was walking briskly across the ballroom toward the band.

Nancy grabbed a canapé from a passing waiter's tray and set off after her. "Here we go," she said to herself. "I just hope I can catch Ms. Ciardi saying or doing something that will help me find Dad."

But after following Gabriella Ciardi around for an hour, Nancy was unable to come up with any useful information. Discouraged, she ordered a glass of ginger ale from the bar and sat down wearily at a table.

Bess plopped down beside her after a moment. "I *finally* got away from that Mrs. Tremain person," she gasped, rolling her eyes. "I can't believe anyone could talk so much!"

"I can't believe it, either," Nancy said with a grin.

Bess glanced around. "What are you doing here all by yourself?" she asked. "Where are George and your aunt Eloise?"

Nancy told Bess how she and George had stumbled upon Gabriella Ciardi and Julian St. James in the midst of an argument. "George is following Mr. St. James," she explained. "I've been tailing Ms. Ciardi. And Aunt Eloise is still following Cassie, I assume." She added, "Oh, by the way, Quito Messenger is here, too. I ran into him a little while ago."

Bess groaned. "Great! I get stuck with Ms. Motor Mouth and miss out on all the action." Then she said, "So you really think Ms. Ciardi and Mr. St. James might be guilty of something major?"

"I don't know," Nancy said slowly. "I still don't

110

have much proof against Mr. St. James—and I have zero proof against Ms. Ciardi. I was hoping I'd overhear her saying something incriminating to somebody, but so far her only topics of conversation have been fashion, fashion, and fashion."

Then Nancy thought of something. She opened her purse and pulled out the pair of red, cat's-eye sunglasses she'd found in her father's hotel suite. "I totally forgot this afternoon to give these to Officer Jordan," she said. "Now I'm wondering— could these belong to Ms. Ciardi? They're an expensive designer brand, which would fit her image. And she's about the same height as the woman we saw."

Bess's eyes lit up. "If these are hers," she said excitedly, "then maybe she was the one who broke into your dad's hotel suite!"

"Which could mean that she's one of Dad's kidnappers," Nancy added, nodding. "I still can't figure out what the break-in had to do with his kidnapping, but—"

Just then a voice broke into their conversation.

"Hey, what are you doing with my sunglasses?"

Nancy glanced up, startled. Cassie Dake stood in front of her and Bess.

"Those are my sunglasses," Cassie declared. "Where did you find them?"

13

The Falcon Connection

Nancy held up the sunglasses. "These are yours?" she asked Cassie slowly. Out of the corner of her eye, she could see her aunt hovering discreetly in the background, a few feet behind Cassie.

"Yeah," Cassie replied. "I just noticed this morning that they were missing. Where did you find them?"

Nancy and Bess exchanged a glance. Nancy wasn't sure how to reply to Cassie's question. Did she have enough evidence to accuse Cassie of breaking into her father's hotel suite and being one of his kidnappers? Or should she make up a story about where she'd found the sunglasses and continue to build a case against Cassie?

Just then a dark-haired young guy came rushing up to Cassie. "Major emergency," he said breathlessly. "The band claims that they were hired to play till nine, not ten o'clock."

"Oh, great," Cassie muttered. She grabbed the sunglasses from Nancy, gave her a brief smile, then turned to go. "I've got to run. Thanks for finding these."

"Wait a second," Nancy said, hastily rising to her feet. "I need those sunglasses back—"

But Cassie appeared not to hear her. She hurried across the ballroom toward the band.

"Oh, great," Nancy muttered, frustrated. "Those sunglasses are a key piece of evidence. How am I going to get them back?"

"I don't know," Bess said. "In any case, I take back what I said before. Cassie could definitely be one of your dad's kidnappers. Those sunglasses are pretty serious proof."

"They sure are," Nancy said. "The question is, who's her accomplice—or accomplices? I'm sure the gray-haired man is involved somehow."

Bess took a sip of Nancy's ginger ale. "So how do we figure out who the kidnappers are and find your dad?" she asked.

"Good question," Nancy said. She felt her heart sink. "We'd better come up with something—and fast. The kidnappers are going to figure out soon enough that we don't have a quarter of a million dollars, and when that happens . . ." Her voice trailed off grimly.

* * *

"That was a lovely party," Aunt Eloise remarked as she, Nancy, Bess, and George debarked from the *Serena*. "I would have had a wonderful time, except that I couldn't stop thinking about Carson."

Nancy hooked her arm through her aunt's. "I know what you mean," she murmured. "I couldn't stop thinking about him, either."

The foursome left the marina, crossed a busy road, and soon found themselves on a quiet street lined with elegant old brownstones. After the loud and lively *Bellissima* party, the quiet seemed especially pronounced. "This neighborhood is called Chelsea," Aunt Eloise explained. "My neighborhood is just south of here."

The group walked in silence for a few moments. The air was blissfully balmy, and there was a full moon in the sky. But Nancy was too distracted to enjoy the spring night. All she could think about was catching her father's kidnappers.

Nancy's aunt interrupted her thoughts. "I forgot to tell you—I did get one piece of information while I was following Cassie around," she said. "Her address. She's having a small, private party at her apartment later tonight, and she was letting people know where she lived."

"Good job, Aunt Eloise," Nancy told her.

"I didn't even get that much out of following Julian St. James for three hours," George grumbled. "I think he was definitely on his guard after running into us, Nan."

Aunt Eloise stopped and pointed to a tall iron gate up ahead. "That's the Hilliard College campus," she said. "I don't usually walk this way, but let's cut through—it's a shortcut to my apartment."

The four of them walked through the iron gate. On the other side were a dozen ivy-covered dormitory and classroom buildings overlooking a grassy quadrangle. Even at this hour of the night there were many students sitting on stone benches or strolling around.

"It must be fun being a college student in Manhattan," Bess said enviously. "Think of all the shopping you could do between classes."

Just then George grabbed Nancy's arm. "Nan—look!"

Nancy glanced up.

George was pointing at a huge red banner hanging over one of the Hilliard buildings. In the center of it was a picture of a falcon—its wings folded, its head turned to the left.

Nancy gasped. "That's just like the picture of the falcon we found in Dad's suite!" she exclaimed.

"Exactly," George murmured.

Nancy moved closer to the banner and studied it intently. "That must be the Hilliard logo," she said excitedly. "Does that mean Dad's disappearance is connected to this place somehow?"

Aunt Eloise, George, and Bess came up beside Nancy. "This case is getting weirder and weirder," Bess remarked. "We've got this huge list of suspects, and now we've got a college logo. What does it all mean?"

"Maybe Dad was working on some big case involving Hilliard College," Nancy guessed. "Ms. Hanson will know—I'll call her first thing tomorrow morning."

"Your father was definitely not working on a case involving Hilliard College," Ms. Hanson told Nancy on Sunday morning. "If he had been, I certainly would have known about it."

Nancy felt a surge of disappointment. She leaned back on the couch and took a sip of her freshly squeezed orange juice. "How about old cases? Do you know if he ever worked on anything involving Hilliard?"

"Not that I can recall," Ms. Hanson replied. "I'm sorry I can't help you." She added, "How are things going? Are you any closer to finding out what happened to your father?"

"We've got some leads," Nancy said vaguely. "I'll let you know the second he turns up." She didn't want to tell Ms. Hanson about the kidnapping angle.

The two of them chatted for a few more minutes, then said goodbye. Nancy was just about to hang up when Ms. Hanson's voice rang out. "Nancy, wait a second! I just thought of something. This may be nothing, but . . ."

"What is it?" Nancy asked her intently.

"Well, your father used to have a client who was an alum of Hilliard College. Desmond Foster," Ms. Hanson explained. "He graduated from there about twenty years ago, I believe. I remember this because my cousin Betsy was a Hilliard alum, too, and we had a conversation about it once."

"Dad *used* to have him as a client?" Nancy said. "I don't understand."

"Mr. Foster died just last week after a sudden illness," Ms. Hanson said.

Nancy was silent as she considered this. "Do you think Dad might have had some business in New York having to do with Mr. Foster?" she said after a moment.

"I don't think so," Ms. Hanson replied. "Mr. Drew's work for him consisted of very straightforward will and estate matters. None of it involved anyone or anything in New York."

After hanging up, Nancy took another sip of her orange juice and considered what Ms. Hanson had told her. It didn't sound as though her father had come to New York on business concerning Hilliard College—or Desmond Foster, for that matter. But she couldn't ignore the fact that he'd drawn a picture of the falcon below the list of five names. What was the connection?

Then something clicked in her mind. She sprang up from the couch. "I just remembered something," she announced to Bess, George, and

Aunt Eloise, who were finishing up their breakfasts at the dining-room table. "I can't believe I forgot about this!"

"What, Nan?" Bess asked her curiously.

"Julian St. James went to Hilliard!" Nancy said excitedly. "When I searched through his office yesterday, I saw a Hilliard alumni magazine on his desk!"

"That's pretty big news," George agreed. "What does it all mean?"

"I'm not sure, but I plan to find out." Nancy glanced at her watch. "Let's go over to the Gotham Theater. Since it's Sunday morning, I'm sure there's no rehearsal going on, so the building's probably empty. I want to search Mr. St. James's office some more."

She turned to her aunt. "Aunt Eloise, you said you found out where Cassie lives," she went on. "Can you go over there and hang out by her building? And follow her if she goes anyplace?"

"Sure thing," Aunt Eloise told her. "Are you thinking now that Julian St. James and Cassie are your kidnappers?"

"I feel pretty sure the gray-haired man is involved," Nancy said. "Otherwise, our only two pieces of physical evidence, the handkerchief and the sunglasses, point to Mr. St. James and Cassie." She added, "Quito and Gabriella Ciardi might be involved, too, but I'm not so sure about them. Right now I just want to get the goods on Mr. St. James and Cassie."

118

Half an hour later Nancy, Bess, and George were in the alley next to the Gotham Theater. Nancy worked quickly to pick open the side door lock, and they went inside.

Nancy tilted her head, listening closely. "This place seems to be totally deserted," she said in a low voice. "I wonder why the hall light's on, though?"

"It's probably always on," Bess told her. "Come on, let's hurry up. What if some janitor shows up or something?"

Nancy walked out into the hallway and turned left toward Julian St. James's office. Then she heard something that sent chills down her spine.

Somewhere in the distance, a male voice was saying: "That girl knows too much about what we did. We've got to kill her—and fast."

14

Closing In

Bess gasped and turned to Nancy. "Mr. St. James is here!" she whispered frantically. "Do you think he's talking about you?"

"That didn't sound like his voice," Nancy whispered back. "Come on—let's check it out."

"Maybe we should just get out of here," George suggested nervously.

"If we're really quiet, he'll never know we're here—whoever he is," Nancy reassured her.

She slipped off her shoes and began walking stealthily in the direction from which the voice had come: the auditorium. George and Bess followed her, also without their shoes. The voice stopped, and an eerie silence hung over the darkened theater. Nancy's heart was pounding. Was she about to come face-to-face with one of her father's kidnappers—a kidnapper with murder on his mind?

They reached the door leading to the auditorium. Nancy pressed her ear against it, and heard nothing. She opened the door as quietly and carefully as possible, then went in. The auditorium was dark, although a dim light shone from the stage.

"Who's there?"

Her senses on full alert, Nancy glanced up at the stage.

Quito was sitting on one of the couches. Seeing Nancy and her friends, he sprang up, looking angry. "What are you all doing here?" he demanded, fists clenched. "And how did you get in?"

"What are *you* doing here?" Nancy countered. At the moment she wasn't sure whether to be scared of Quito or not.

"I came in to do some rehearsing on my own," Quito replied with a frown. "As if it were any business of yours. Now, as I said before, what are you all doing here?"

Nancy realized in an instant that the menacing words she and her friends had overheard must have been a line from the play. Breathing a sigh of relief, she turned to Quito and said, "We're looking for Mr. St. James."

"He's not here." Quito eyed her warily. "Why are you always after him, anyway? What's going on?"

Nancy's mind raced as she tried to think of a good cover story. But after a moment's thought, she decided to go for the truth instead. If Quito was one of the kidnappers, she reasoned, his reaction might give him away. If he weren't, she had nothing to lose.

Nancy took a deep breath, then said, "My father, Carson Drew, came to New York last Sunday. Sometime Tuesday afternoon he disappeared without a trace. We haven't heard from him since. He had an appointment with Mr. St. James on Tuesday at three o'clock, so on Friday we came by to ask him about it. Mr. St. James said Dad never showed up. He also said the only reason he gave Dad the appointment was because he thought he was some guy named Carl Drew.

"I think Mr. St. James was lying," she went on. "First, we found a handkerchief in his office that looked like one of Dad's. Second, there's no Carl Drew in Mr. St. James's address book. And third, Dad left a clue in his hotel suite that had something to do with Hilliard College, where Mr. St. James went."

Quito was silent for a long moment, apparently considering something. Then he came down the steps and joined the girls on the floor. He had a troubled expression on his face.

Watching him, Nancy had a sudden, powerful instinct that he wasn't one of the kidnappers but knew something about her dad's disappearance.

"If you know anything about my father—anything at all—please tell us," she pleaded with him.

Quito stared at her, then said, "I think I know something that might help you out. I didn't want to say anything because I didn't want to get Julian in trouble. He was nice enough to give me a shot at this play. *Deadly Secrets* is my first Broadway gig. It's really, really important to my career—do you understand?"

"We understand," Nancy said quickly. "But I think you can understand how important it is to me to get my father back, safe and sound."

Quito nodded. "Okay, here's the scoop," he said. "Last Tuesday, around two-thirty, Julian cut rehearsal short and told everyone to go home. But I stuck around for a while because I was meeting a friend in the neighborhood."

"Did Mr. St. James know you were here?" Bess asked him.

Quito shook his head. "No. Anyway, around three I saw some dude—tall, dark hair, maybe around forty or so—walk in the front door. Julian came right out and took him back to his office. I heard the guy introduce himself as Carson Drew."

Nancy gasped. "So Dad *was* here! I just knew it!"

"The two of them never saw me—I was in the wings," Quito went on. "Anyway, I didn't think anything of it until Friday, when you three came by. I was outside Julian's office waiting to talk to him and overheard you asking if your dad was here on Tuesday at three. When Julian lied and said no, I knew something weird was up."

Nancy's mind was racing. "Did you see my dad leave this place?" she asked Quito.

"Nope. After I saw Julian take your dad back to his office, I decided to cut out and get something to eat," Quito replied.

"Mr. St. James said that the blue handkerchief we found belonged to Carl Drew, one of the show's backers," George spoke up. "Do you know if there's such a person?"

"As far as I know, there's only one person paying for this show—some rich old woman named Mrs. Bullard," Quito said. "I think Julian was lying."

Nancy went on to describe Cassie Dake and the gray-haired man who'd been following the girls, and asked Quito if he knew either of them. He said no. She then asked if he'd ever seen Mr. St. James with Gabriella Ciardi. Quito said he'd spotted them together only once—at the *Bellissima* party.

"Speaking of the *Bellissima* party, what were you doing there?" Nancy asked him curiously.

Quito looked embarrassed. "I wanted to make some contacts," he explained. "I'm trying to get into some modeling on the side. The thing is, I didn't have an invite—I just heard about the party through the grapevine. So I had to crash."

"Do you have any idea where Mr. St. James is now?" Nancy asked him.

"I'm guessing he's out at his beach house in Southampton," Quito said. "He usually spends Sundays there. Julian had the cast out there a few weeks ago. It's a cool place—real secluded and all."

The word *secluded* jolted something in Nancy's brain. A secluded beach house would be a perfect place for St. James to have hidden her father!

Nancy glanced at her watch—it was after ten o'clock. "If we can catch a train soon, we could be out there in a few hours," she said.

Quito dipped a hand into his jeans pocket and fished out a ring of keys. "I have a better idea— why don't I drive you? I've got a car, and it's parked right outside. It's not in the greatest shape, but it works."

"Great," Nancy said eagerly. "But we have to hurry. I have a feeling my father may be out there—and I have a feeling he's in trouble."

Two and a half hours later Quito, Nancy, George, and Bess drove into the ritzy beach community of Southampton, toward the far end of Long Island. The main street was lined with boutiques, cafés, and restaurants. Because it was April, there were few people around.

"I'm pretty sure this is how to get to the house," Quito said, turning onto a road that ran along the ocean.

Nancy rolled down the window. A cool, salty breeze blew in, stirring her hair. Staring at the silver-gray ocean, she thought that it was both beautiful and forlorn-looking. Except for some seagulls, the beach was deserted.

George's voice cut into her thoughts. "Hey, Nan? Do you really think we'll find your dad at Mr. St. James's house?"

"I think it's a strong possibility," Nancy replied. "If Mr. St. James is one of his kidnappers, it would be the perfect place to hide him. It's away from Manhattan, and it sounds as if it's pretty private." She added, "I don't get why he would kidnap Dad, though. He seems to have plenty of money. He must have some other motive."

Quito's car made a sputtering noise. "What's that?" Bess said, alarmed.

"Oh, it's nothing. As you can see, this baby isn't exactly brand-new." Quito ran a loving hand across the dirty, ripped-up dashboard. The rest of the car wasn't in much better shape; the exterior was rusty and in desperate need of a paint job.

Quito continued down the road. They passed a number of expensive-looking beach properties, but as they went on, the road became increasingly less populated.

Just then the car made a louder sputtering noise, then it ground to a halt altogether. "Uh-oh," Quito muttered.

Nancy frowned. "Is it dead?"

Quito shifted gears and turned the key in the ignition. The car squealed but didn't start up again. "Yup," he said heavily. "It's definitely dead."

"Can we call a tow truck?" Bess suggested.

"I don't remember passing a garage," Quito replied. "I've got some tools in the back—maybe I can deal with it."

"I know a little something about cars—I could help you," George offered.

Nancy leaned forward in her seat. "How far is St. James's house from here?"

"I think it's about a mile down this road," Quito explained. "There's a sign hanging in front of it that says 'Seabreeze.' You can't miss it."

Nancy turned to Bess, who was sitting next to her. "You and I can walk down there while these two fix the car," she said. "If this guy has Dad, I don't want to waste another second."

"Um, sure, whatever," Bess said, sounding less than enthusiastic. "Just promise me that we won't do anything dangerous, okay?"

Nancy and Bess reached the Broadway director's house twenty minutes later. Seabreeze was a large, rambling white house overlooking the ocean. Set back from the road, it had a brambly, overgrown lawn, which lent the place a certain wild charm. The nearest property was at least a hundred yards away.

Nancy stood at the front gate with Bess, studying the layout. "All the curtains are drawn," she noted. "And there are a couple of cars parked in the driveway."

"I'll bet Julian St. James is in there with Cassie and that nasty, gray-haired man," Bess said, shivering. "I don't like this, Nan. Maybe we should get the police."

"We don't have enough proof to take to the police—not just yet," Nancy said. "Come on— maybe we can get into the house without anyone noticing."

Nancy and Bess quickly made their way across the lawn, ducking behind trees and bushes as much as possible. When they got to the front door, Nancy tried the knob. It wasn't locked, and no alarm went off. "Bingo," she whispered to Bess. "Okay, follow me."

Nancy opened the door very slowly and found herself in a large foyer. It was decorated simply with wicker furniture, a faded Oriental rug, and nautical prints hanging on the white walls. Nancy listened carefully for sounds—there were none.

A long hallway extended from the foyer. "This way," she whispered to Bess.

Tiptoeing quietly, Nancy kept her ears and eyes open for any signs of St. James. As she and Bess proceeded down the hallway, they passed two closed doors, then a third. At the fourth door Nancy paused. There were muffled voices coming from inside.

She turned to Bess, put a finger to her lips, then

pressed her ear against the door. But at the exact same moment, the door opened.

Julian St. James stood there, his black eyes wide with shock. "What are you—" he began, then glanced nervously over his shoulder.

Nancy followed his glance—and gasped.

Inside the room was her father, tied up in a chair. And standing around him were four familiar faces: Sonny Tremain, Page Durrell, Aristotle Kiriakis, and Gabriella Ciardi!

15

Partners in Crime

"Nancy!" her father cried out in a weak, raspy voice. "Get out of here!"

"Not so fast." Julian St. James grabbed Nancy's and Bess's arms and pulled them roughly into the room. He slammed the door shut and turned the lock.

"There aren't any more of you out there, are there?" St. James asked Nancy.

Without replying, Nancy rushed up to her father and knelt down beside him. Her eyes filled with tears at the sight of his pale, haggard face and his bound wrists and ankles. "Dad—are you okay?"

Carson tried to smile at her, but she could see that it was an effort. "They haven't hurt me, anyway," he replied.

"Not yet," Judge Tremain spoke up. His formerly kind voice now sounded menacing.

Nancy stood up. Bess clung to her elbow, looking terrified. Page Durrell, Aristotle Kiriakis, Gabriella Ciardi, and Julian St. James were hovering in a semicircle around the judge. They all seemed to be staring at him nervously.

Nancy fixed her eyes on Judge Tremain. "What's going on here?" she demanded. "Why are you keeping my father prisoner?"

"Because he and his stupid little client couldn't keep their noses out of other people's business," he replied nastily.

Stupid little client, Nancy thought to herself. What does he mean by that? And then she recalled what Ms. Hanson had told her that morning. Everything became clear to her.

"It's Desmond Foster, isn't it?" she said out loud. "This whole business has something to do with him. And with Hilliard College."

Page Durrell glanced at the judge, her pale blue eyes full of alarm. "She knows, Sonny!" she said in a frightened voice.

"What does it matter that she knows?" Judge Tremain scoffed. "Once we get our hands on the evidence Desmond put together against us, we'll be in the clear. No one will believe the words of some small-town lawyer and a couple of teenagers with overactive imaginations."

Nancy's mind was racing. What was he talking

about? It seemed as though he and the others had committed some crime that Desmond Foster had known about. But now Desmond Foster was dead. Had he given the information to Nancy's dad to turn over to the authorities? And had Judge Tremain and the others kidnapped Carson Drew before he could do so?

Then another, more disturbing thought crossed Nancy's mind.

Had the five of them killed Desmond Foster in order to silence him?

Dr. Kiriakis's voice broke into her thoughts. "Um, Sonny? What are we going to do about these three?" He didn't sound very happy.

"Let's tie up the girls, then discuss the matter elsewhere," Judge Tremain replied. "Julian, do you have any more rope in this shack of yours?" The director nodded and left the room.

"We just need to figure out how to get our hands on Myles's diary and Desmond's letter, and we're home free," the judge went on.

Myles? Who is Myles? Nancy wondered. Out loud, she said, "I still don't understand. How do the five of you know one another?"

"The falcon, my dear—the falcon," Judge Tremain said with a cold smile.

"You all went to Hilliard College," Nancy said slowly. "The five of you, plus Desmond Foster. You were classmates, weren't you?"

The judge clapped. "Bravo! And now this cross-examination session is over."

Julian St. James had returned with a length of rope and a small kitchen knife. Judge Tremain took them from him, then waved the knife at Nancy and Bess. "If you don't want to get hurt, you'll cooperate," he warned. He nodded at two wooden chairs. "Sit down."

Nancy hesitated for a moment, trying to assess the situation. Could she fight back and get herself, Bess, and her father out of the room? It was doubtful—there were five of them to contend with. After a moment she sat down, and Bess followed suit.

Judge Tremain tied them up quickly with Julian St. James's help, then put the knife and remaining rope down on a table. "That should hold them," he said to the others. "Come on—let's go."

Gabriella Ciardi threw him a withering glance. "If this whole unpleasant episode backfires on us, Sonny, you'll be very sorry," she said.

The judge narrowed his eyes at her. "So will you, my dear Gaby," he sneered. "As I've explained to you all many times, I may have been the one who killed Myles Gingrass twenty years ago, but you were all on the sailboat with us that day—you were my accessories after the fact, as they say in the legal world. And furthermore, you've all been involved as much as I have in this little kidnapping business. So don't threaten me, Gaby—if I go down, you'll all go down, too."

Ms. Ciardi glared at him. "Fine. Whatever. Let's just get on with it."

The fivesome left the room and closed the door. Nancy turned to her father. "There are a million questions I want to ask you," she said in a low voice. "But this isn't the time. We have to get out of here."

"Any ideas?" Carson Drew asked his daughter.

Nancy nodded, then began trying to rock her chair toward the table where the judge had left the knife. Fortunately, the floor was carpeted and muffled the sounds of her movements.

"Nan, what are you doing?" Bess whispered.

"I'm going after that knife," Nancy replied tersely.

"Be careful, honey," her dad told her. "They could be back any minute."

Nancy continued her slow, tortuous journey toward the table. It was only five feet away, but with her hands and feet bound, it was hard to make the rocking motion necessary to move her chair toward her goal. And each time she rocked, the ropes dug painfully into her skin.

After a few more minutes she finally reached the table. Realizing that there was no way to pick up the knife with her hands, she bent down and clamped her teeth around the wooden handle. Then she began rocking over to where Bess was sitting.

When she reached Bess, she bent down and dropped the knife on her friend's lap. Then she turned her own chair around so she could pick up the knife with her bound hands. She positioned herself back-to-back with Bess and began sawing at the other girl's bonds.

"Try not to draw too much blood, okay?" Bess whispered nervously.

"I'll go really slowly and carefully," Nancy whispered back.

A short while later Bess said, "I think you've got it. Here, stop sawing for a second."

Nancy did so, and Bess pulled her hands apart. "That did it!" she announced. "I'm free!"

Nancy nodded. "Great. Now untie your ankles, then untie us, too—quickly. Those guys could be back any minute."

Bess freed herself and Nancy, then Nancy freed her dad. Father and daughter exchanged a brief, joyful hug.

Nancy stepped back and studied Carson Drew anxiously. "Can you stand, Dad?"

"I think so." He rose to his feet very tentatively. "For the first few days they were letting me walk around a bit. But since Friday I've pretty much been in this chair. My legs are numb."

"Have they been feeding you?" Nancy asked him worriedly.

Carson Drew nodded. "They needed information from me," he said, "so they couldn't afford to have me starve to death on them. But I'll explain everything later. Right now we have to concentrate on getting out of here."

Nancy ran to the door and listened. She could hear the faint sound of footsteps. "They're coming!'' she whispered frantically. Then she glanced around the room and noticed a large window. Without wasting another second, she dashed over and opened it wide. "Come on, guys—this way!"

Nancy and Bess helped Nancy's dad climb out. Then Bess went, then Nancy. The young detective was jumping onto the lawn when she heard Judge Tremain and the others burst into the room behind her.

"Stop them!" Nancy heard the judge cry out. "They're getting away!"

Nancy put her hand on her father's arm. "Do you think you can run?"

"I don't think I have much of a choice," he replied grimly.

Nancy, Bess, and Mr. Drew sprinted across the lawn. It had begun to rain softly; the air was damp and salty, and a light mist hung over everything. When they were halfway across the lawn, Nancy peered over her shoulder. Judge Tremain and the others were only fifty feet behind them, and closing fast.

Then she glanced at her father. He was managing to keep up with her and Bess, but just barely. Come on, Dad, she urged him silently. You can do it.

But all of a sudden her father stumbled on a dead branch and went tumbling to the ground. "Dad!" Nancy cried out.

She stopped in her tracks and doubled back to help him. But it was too late. Judge Tremain and the others closed in on Carson Drew in a matter of seconds.

The judge grabbed Mr. Drew's arm and pulled him roughly to his feet. "Get up," Tremain said gruffly. "No more fun and games. I'm going to take care of you—all of you—once and for all."

"You leave my father alone—" Nancy began. But her words caught in her throat when she saw the shiny object in Judge Tremain's hand.

It was the kitchen knife.

16

A Secret Is Revealed

Nancy gasped in horror. Did Judge Tremain plan on killing her dad to silence him for good? And her and Bess, too?

Just then she heard the sound of screeching tires and the wail of a police siren.

"Sonny, the police!" Page Durrell cried out hysterically. "What are we going to do?"

"The police? But how?" The judge shook his head in bewilderment. Then he let go of Carson Drew and thrust the kitchen knife in Ms. Durrell's hands. "Page, take this back into the house right away. And as for the rest of you"—he glanced at Julian St. James, Gabriella Ciardi, and Aristotle Kiriakis—"don't say a word when the police get here. Let me deal with them."

A moment later Quito's car pulled up to the front gate, followed by a police car. Quito stopped and got out, followed by George. Nancy, Bess, and Nancy's dad rushed to the gate to join them. The judge and the others made no effort to restrain them.

"Mr. Drew—it's so good to see you!" George exclaimed happily. "Are you guys okay?"

"Yes!" Nancy said breathlessly. "I'm so glad you brought the police!"

Quito grinned sheepishly. "We didn't, um, bring them, exactly. After we got the car fixed, we speeded here the entire way, and I think the dude was just about to give me a ticket."

A middle-aged police officer got out of his car and was ambling toward the group. "Do you know how fast you were going, young man?" he barked at Quito.

"Forget the speeding ticket for now. I want to press charges against the owner of this house and four of his friends," Carson Drew spoke up. "They've been holding me prisoner for the last six days."

At that moment Judge Tremain walked up to the front gate, followed by Ms. Ciardi, Dr. Kiriakis, and Mr. St. James.

"Officer, I'm so glad you're here," the judge said with a charming smile. "Let me introduce myself. I'm Lyman Tremain, a family court judge in Manhattan. Perhaps you've heard of me; I'm running for state attorney general in the fall. My friends and I were having a private party when these people here"—he nodded toward Carson,

Nancy, and Bess—"decided to trespass on Mr. St. James's property—"

"Give it up, Sonny," Carson Drew cut in coldly. "With the evidence I have against you, you and your friends are going to jail for a long, long time."

"And don't forget, Bess and I are witnesses," Nancy added.

The judge stared at Nancy and her dad, opened his mouth, then clamped it shut.

"Sonny, this is all your fault!" Ms. Ciardi screeched.

"I want to hear the whole story," Aunt Eloise said.

She, George, Bess, Nancy and Nancy's dad were sitting around her living room Sunday evening. Cartons of take-out Chinese food filled the coffee table. The blinds were open, and the night view of downtown Manhattan was breathtaking.

Carson Drew, who'd spent the afternoon talking to the police and being examined by a doctor, turned to his sister. "Aren't you hungry? You haven't touched any of this delicious food."

"I'm too happy to be hungry," Aunt Eloise replied, her eyes misting with tears. "I thought I'd never see you again, Carson."

He squeezed her shoulder. "Well, here I am, good as new." He turned to the others. "As for the story—where to begin?"

"Maybe with Desmond Foster," Nancy prompted him. She, Bess, and George had heard the entire account at the police station. It was an amazing tale, and Nancy was still trying to absorb it.

"Yes, Desmond Foster." Carson put his chopsticks down. "Desmond Foster was a client of mine—had been, for a long time. He fell sick very recently—a fast-growing form of leukemia—and about two weeks ago he called me to his deathbed. He said that he wanted to confess something to me, plus ask me to do a very large favor."

Aunt Eloise raised her eyebrows. "A favor?"

"Desmond explained that twenty years ago he and five of his classmates at Hilliard—Sonny, Julian, Gabriella, Page, and Aristotle—did a terrible thing," Mr. Drew went on. "One spring afternoon their senior year, they went out sailing with another friend, Myles Gingrass, who was Desmond's roommate. Sonny and Myles got into a fistfight, and Sonny punched him so hard that Myles went overboard."

"Oh, dear!" Aunt Eloise gasped.

"Sonny told the others not to go in after him," Nancy's dad said. "He figured Myles would be able to drag himself aboard on his own. The others listened to him—they were all intimidated by him." He sighed and shook his head. "A few minutes passed, and Myles didn't surface. Finally Sonny realized something was wrong, and dived in. But he never found Myles's body. Apparently Sonny's punch had knocked Myles unconscious. The poor guy never had a chance."

141

"How awful!" Eloise said.

Nancy took up the story. "Sonny Tremain ordered the others not to say anything about it to the authorities. He came from a rich family, and he had major career aspirations. He was afraid something like this would get him into terrible trouble."

"The others went along," George continued. "None of them wanted to get into trouble, either. Weeks later Myles Gingrass's body washed up on the beach. Since nobody came forward with any information, it was ruled as an accidental drowning."

"But there *was* a piece of evidence that could hurt them all big-time," Bess said, waving her chopsticks in the air for emphasis. "Desmond Foster found Myles Gingrass's diary in the room they shared at Hilliard. In the diary there was an entry for the day they all went sailing. Myles Gingrass wrote that he planned to go sailing with his five friends that afternoon, but that he was worried about seeing Sonny Tremain. They hadn't been getting along lately." She added, "Myles Gingrass even wrote something about Sonny Tremain's violent temper."

Carson Drew took up the story again. "Desmond kept the diary all these years," he said. "He couldn't bring himself to turn it in to the authorities, but he couldn't bring himself to destroy it, either. When he found himself dying, he realized that he had to tell the truth—that withholding information about a crime was not only illegal but wrong. So he gave me Myles's diary. He also wrote a letter in my presence in which he described everything that happened twenty years ago. He asked that I hand the diary and the letter over to the authorities in New York."

"And did you?" Aunt Eloise asked him.

Mr. Drew shook his head. "Not right away," he admitted. "I wanted to confront Sonny, Gabriella, Julian, Page, and Aristotle and give them a chance to turn themselves in. The whole matter was a very delicate one, after all—they're very successful, prominent citizens, especially Sonny."

Aunt Eloise looked confused. "But you didn't meet with any of the five, right? At least, that's what they said."

"They were lying," Nancy told her aunt. "They all gave Dad appointments as soon as he explained what he wanted to see them about."

Her dad nodded. "My first two appointments were with Sonny and Gabriella," he explained. "Both of them acted as though they would cooperate, but they were just pretending. By the time I got to my meeting with Julian on Tuesday afternoon, they were all in a full panic. None of them wanted the truth to come out."

"So they decided to kidnap you," Aunt Eloise said, shivering. "Where did it happen?"

"At the Gotham Theater, during my meeting with Julian," he said. "A little chloroform, and I was out like a light. The next thing I knew, I was at

Julian's Southampton house with all five of them. They said they'd let me go if I would just hand over the originals of Myles's diary and Desmond's letter." He shrugged. "Of course, I refused."

Nancy took a bite of sweet-and-sour shrimp, then said, "When I showed up in town, found the list in Dad's hotel suite, and started calling the five people for appointments, they all freaked out. Only Judge Tremain was level-headed enough to give me an appointment—he wanted to see how much I knew. Of course, he lied about meeting with Dad. And when I left there, he called the others and told them they had to meet with me, too, so as not to arouse suspicions."

Nancy added, "I should have noticed this before, but when I first called Ms. Ciardi, Ms. Durrell, and Mr. St. James, I didn't leave a phone number with them. And yet they somehow managed to call me back. See, they got the number from Judge Tremain."

"The judge also put a tail on us," Bess said. "That gray-haired man was a private detective Judge Tremain hired to follow us around town. I guess the judge wanted to make sure he knew all our movements."

"What about the woman with the red sunglasses?" Aunt Eloise asked. "Was that Cassie?"

"That was Gabriella Ciardi," George replied. "The business with the sunglasses really threw us."

Bess nodded. "The sunglasses belonged to

Cassie, but Ms. Ciardi borrowed them on Thursday, which Cassie totally forgot about. On Thursday night Ms. Ciardi headed over to the Imperial Hotel, sort of in disguise. She had Mr. Drew's key, and she was to search his hotel suite for the diary and letter. She had no idea that they were back in River Heights, in Mr. Drew's safe."

"When Ms. Ciardi tried to get into Dad's hotel suite, she ran into George and me," Nancy went on. "But she succeeded on Friday—that's why Dad's suite was such a mess." She added, "Cassie never had anything to do with anything. She was totally innocent."

"So was Quito," Bess said. "And Miguel Lopez."

"What about the call we got on Friday night?" Aunt Eloise said, puzzled. "Who was behind that?"

"That was Judge Tremain," Nancy explained. "He got the idea to call us and pretend to be some anonymous kidnapper who was after money. He thought that would throw us off the track."

Bess leaned forward. "Oh, and remember that suit of armor thing?" she said. "That was Page Durrell trying to scare us off the case. She was really clever about it, too—she pretended to have a sprained ankle so we'd never suspect her of beating us to the Arms and Armor room."

"And Dr. Kiriakis was responsible for locking us in the morgue on Saturday," George said. "He deliberately told the receptionist to direct us to the wrong room, and when we were in there, he locked it from outside. He was trying to scare us off the case, too."

Aunt Eloise shook her head in amazement. "What an incredible story! A twenty-year-old mystery, a dying man's confession, a kidnapping, nasty business with suits of armors and morgues . . ." She turned to her brother. "Will Sonny and the others be prosecuted for what they did to Myles Gingrass?"

"Probably," he replied. "At the very least, Sonny will be charged with manslaughter, and the others will be charged with being accessories after the fact. And of course, there's the new charge of kidnapping." He added, "They would all have been better off dealing with what they did to Myles when it happened. But they were too concerned with saving their necks."

"My guess is that, if it hadn't been for Judge Tremain, the others would have gone to the police long ago," Nancy said. "He managed to convince them to cover up the Myles Gingrass incident—just as he convinced them that they had to kidnap Dad before the truth got out."

"Well, now the truth *is* out, thanks to you," Aunt Eloise said, beaming at Nancy's dad.

"I might not have lived long enough to tell it if it hadn't been for the four of you." Carson Drew put his arm around Nancy's shoulders and smiled lovingly at her. "Especially you."

Nancy smiled back at him. "I'm just glad you're back with us, Dad."

"I love happy endings," Bess gushed. She reached for a fortune cookie and cracked it open. "Hey, listen to this, guys! 'You must work less and play more.' I think that means we need to take a break from all this detective stuff and have some fun in the Big Apple!"

"Actually, I've had all the excitement I can handle for a while," Mr. Drew told her with a grin. "What I really need is a good dose of home, sweet home."

THE HARDY BOYS® SERIES By Franklin W. Dixon

**LOOK FOR
AN EXCITING NEW
HARDY BOYS MYSTERY
COMING FROM
MINSTREL® BOOKS**